A Note of Secrecy

As Karen pushed Ben's notebooks aside, the edge of a pale pink envelope fell out. Karen's heart pounded as she stared at it. It seemed to glow against the cafeteria table, mocking her.

She pulled the pink envelope farther out, and it said exactly what she'd been afraid of. "Emily Van Patten, New York City."

Karen felt like crying. Even though Ben had been in love with Emily, he was dating Karen now. All Karen's old insecurities came rushing back when she thought of Emily Van Patten. Emily was tall, blond, and beautiful, a successful model. Karen just couldn't compete with her.

Karen had been so thrilled to be dating Ben that she hadn't wondered too much about his old love. Maybe it was time she did.

Her heart beat faster with fear. Was Ben still in love with Emily Van Patten?

Books in the RIVER HEIGHTS ™ Series

Available from ARCHWAY Paperbacks

RIVER HEIGHTS™ #8

THE TROUBLE WITH LOVE

CAROLYN KEENE

AN ARCHWAY PAPERBACK
Published by POCKET BOOKS
New York   London   Toronto   Sydney   Tokyo   Singapore

AN ARCHWAY PAPERBACK *Original*

An Archway Paperback published by
POCKET BOOKS, a division of Simon & Schuster Inc.
1230 Avenue of the Americas, New York, NY 10020

ISBN: 0-671-67766-7

First Archway Paperback printing November 1990

10 9 8 7 6 5 4 3 2 1

Cover illustration by Carla Sormanti

Printed in the U.S.A.

IL 6 +

THE TROUBLE WITH LOVE

 **1**

"I'm sorry, Rick," Lacey Dupree murmured, twisting her fingers together in her lap. "I never should have believed Brittany Tate's accusations for one second. I should have known you'd never be involved in that cheating ring. Please, please forgive me."

She was looking at her boyfriend, Rick Stratton, who couldn't answer her. His eyes were closed, and his face was almost as white as the crisp hospital sheet pulled up to his chest. He was unconscious and had been since his rock-climbing accident Thursday night. Lacey had been there late the night before with Rick's family until they'd been asked to leave. That Monday, she'd raced over from school as soon as the last bell had rung.

Once in a while Rick's glazed eyes would open, but he never seemed to recognize her. Still, Lacey would try to get through to him. She had to talk to him the second he woke up. He'd open his eyes, and—

But what would his expression be? Suddenly Lacey stood up and walked to the window. She pressed her forehead against the cool pane and stared with blank eyes out at the parking lot. He would hate her, she knew it! If she hadn't accused him of being involved in the River Heights High cheating scandal, they wouldn't have had that big fight. He never would have rushed off that way. He wouldn't have been distracted when he went rock climbing. He wouldn't have fallen, and he wouldn't be lying in a hospital bed, unconscious.

A sob broke loose, and Lacey pressed a fist to her mouth. Tears streamed down her cheeks. "Please wake up, Rick," she whispered.

Behind her she heard the whoosh of the door. Quickly Lacey wiped the tears off her face and turned around. Rick's mother was standing beside the door.

"Lacey, honey, why don't you go home and rest. It's almost dinnertime." Mrs. Stratton smiled. Her hazel eyes were so like Rick's that they brought a new rush of pain to Lacey.

Lacey tried to smile back. "I'd like to stay a few more minutes, Mrs. Stratton. If you don't mind, that is."

"Of course, honey." Mrs. Stratton sat on a plastic chair next to the one Lacey took. "Hello, Rick," she said, taking his hand. "I'm taking a leave of absence from work so I can visit you more often. Everybody at home misses you. Last night your aunt Elise called, and . . ."

Lacey tuned Mrs. Stratton out. It broke her heart to hear Rick's mother talk to him as though he were awake and could hear her. The doctors were afraid Rick would slide into a coma, and his mother felt that if she kept talking Rick would hear her and want to return to all of them, to his life.

Mrs. Stratton smiled a shaky smile at Rick and smoothed his sheet. "Let's see. Your father is leaving work early, so he'll be here soon." Tears gathered on her lashes.

Lacey wanted to run out of the room, but she forced herself to remain. Rick's mother loved him so much, and she was so nice to Lacey, too. What would she do if she knew that it was Lacey's fault her son was lying there in the first place?

"Just look at that Karen Jacobs!" exclaimed Kim Bishop. She flipped angrily through a rack of clothes in Glad Rags. "Ever since she and Ben Newhouse became an item she's had her nose in the air. She acts as if they're the hottest couple at River Heights High." She tossed her smooth blond hair back and plucked a pink blouse off the rack to add to the pile of clothes on her arm.

Brittany Tate narrowed her dark eyes and glanced across the store. Karen was standing at a mirror, deciding on a new leather jacket. Kim was right—going out with Ben Newhouse had gone to Karen's head.

Brittany opened her mouth to say her thought out loud, but she quickly closed it. She'd almost forgotten—she was a whole new person now. She'd made a resolution that morning at school to be nice. A mean remark hadn't passed her lips all day. She couldn't spoil it now.

Brittany's dark eyes sparkled and her full lips curved into a smile as she thought of several cutting remarks she could deliver. She could zing Karen and Kim at the same time. Kim, one of her best friends, had become conceited, too, since she had a new boyfriend—Jeremy Pratt, the biggest snob at school.

But instead Brittany turned to Kim with a sincere expression. "You and Jeremy are still the hottest topic around school. *That's* not going to change."

Kim eyed her suspiciously, but there

hadn't been the slightest tinge of sarcasm in Brittany's remark. Kim turned her attention back to the clothes rack. "I just hope Karen doesn't get the better of you, Brittany. Before you know it they'll be deciding who'll be editor in chief of the *Record* next year. Even though Karen didn't write the article on the cheating scandal at school, she was the one who found out about it first, wasn't she?"

"She happened to overhear a conversation," Brittany said. "It was pure luck, and journalism is a lot more than luck. I was the one who broke the story. Now the cheating ring has been smashed to smithereens, and I'm the one who did it."

"Right," Kim stated. "And the basketball team probably won't do very well now. Because of the scandal Coach Shay was fired and Jerry Kuperman has to sit out three games."

Brittany shrugged. "Jerry should be punished. He was the ringleader. Coach Shay definitely turned a blind eye to what was going on. The school is better off without him. I'm going to do a follow-up article on the pressures of high school athletics. DeeDee thinks it's a fantastic idea."

"And it just might make you editor in chief." Kim smirked.

Brittany flipped past several dresses on the clothes rack. If she had to bite her tongue any more, it might bleed. She took her job on the *Record* seriously. She hated it when Kim hinted that Brittany only liked the paper because of the power and glory that went along with it.

Kim slid a yellow print blouse off the rack to study it. The color made Brittany's skin crawl. Could Kim really be considering it?

"Karen just might get the nod, anyway," Kim went on idly. "She's still DeeDee's favorite, isn't she?" Kim held the blouse up for Brittany's inspection. "What do you think? Jeremy loves me in yellow."

Buy it, Kim, Brittany thought. It's gorgeous. That color would make Kim's skin look like the cafeteria's pea soup. She deserved it, after that remark about Karen. But no, Brittany had to be good. "Well, it's nice. But I'm not sure about the color."

Kim frowned. "You're right." She slid the blouse back onto the rack.

"Have you heard any more about Rick Stratton?" Kim asked suddenly. "I heard he might go into a coma," she added in a low tone.

Brittany jumped. "What? I don't believe it!" she exclaimed in a shrill voice.

Kim cocked an eyebrow at her. "Well, we all want Rick to get better, of course. Especially Lacey Dupree. She hasn't left his side except to sleep and go to school. She's carrying this angel-of-mercy bit too far, don't you think?"

"Don't be silly, Kim. Lacey's just worried about Rick. Why don't you try on that gorgeous blue sweater? I'll wait here." Brittany practically pushed Kim toward a dressing room.

"Okay," Kim agreed. "But look around some more for me, okay?"

"Sure. Go ahead, Kim." Brittany watched, relieved, as Kim disappeared into a dressing room.

If only she hadn't hinted to Lacey that Rick was involved in the cheating ring! She hadn't known anything for sure. Brittany had information that a "Rick S." was involved. How could she have known it would turn out to be Rick Sutton? It *could* have been Rick Stratton. And if it had been, Lacey would have been better off knowing before the whole school did.

She didn't know the two of them would get into such a huge fight. Brittany stared at the rack of dresses and forced herself to be honest. She *had* hoped they'd fight. But she hadn't wanted anyone to get hurt.

It was all her fault that Rick might never regain consciousness. He might go into a coma! Well, she'd schemed and manipulated and stretched the truth—no, lied, Brittany amended firmly—for the very last time.

A new Brittany Tate would emerge from this disaster. She'd be incredibly sweet and nice. She wouldn't let a mean remark pass her lips, and she'd never flirt again. She'd even out-saint Nikki Masters. Now *that* would take some doing. Brittany hoped she wouldn't become as boring as Nikki.

A hand tugged at her sleeve. "Are you going to beam back to earth anytime soon, Brittany?" Samantha Daley asked, her cinnamon brown eyes open wide. "I called your name three times."

"Oh. Hi, Samantha. I didn't hear you."

"I'll say. What were you thinking about?"

"Where have you been?" Brittany asked, sidestepping Samantha's question. "You were supposed to meet us an hour ago."

"I said I'd *try* to meet you." Samantha picked up a pink chiffon scarf and let it drift through her fingers. "I was with Kyle," she said. "I just left him at the computer store."

Kyle Kirkwood was Samantha's latest conquest. He'd been a brainy social zero with bad clothes and a terrible haircut before Samantha had made him over. Now he was a brainy social zero with cool clothes and a great haircut.

Kim pranced out of the dressing room in the blue sweater. She struck a dramatic pose for them. "Am I hot, or what?"

"You're hot," Brittany said glumly.

"Fabulous sweater," Samantha agreed.

Normally they'd share a conspiratorial look at Kim's conceited attitude, so Brittany didn't dare look at Samantha. It wasn't nice to roll your eyes behind someone's back, Brittany reminded herself.

Kim peered out the Glad Rags window into the mall. "Check that out. Is that Lara Bennett with Kyle?"

Samantha's curly brown hair flew as her head snapped up. "Lara Bennett? She's a sophomore!"

"So?" Kim asked, still peering out the window. "She's cute. It looks like your makeover was a big success, Samantha. Are you sure you didn't go too far, though?"

Quickly Samantha went to the window and peered out. She stared at Kyle and Lara for a minute, then shrugged. "I'm not worried," she said. "Kyle is crazy about me. And Lara is still kind of wimpy—even after the makeover you did for her, Brittany."

"I think Lara is a lovely person," Brittany said, and she meant it.

Kim and Samantha exchanged incredulous looks. Then Kim's cool blue eyes narrowed. "Oh, I get it."

"Get what?" Brittany asked suspiciously.

"You've been acting weird all day. But you're just up to your old tricks," Kim said with a superior smile. She turned to

Samantha. "We should have put the facts together."

Samantha nodded vigorously. "You're right. What facts?"

Kim ticked off the answers on her long fingers. "One, Nikki Masters and Tim Cooper have broken up. Two, there's no way this is temporary since Nikki is hanging all over that new English guy, Niles Butler. Three, Tim is up for grabs—and we all know his type."

"Right," Samantha agreed again. "Nikki Masters."

Kim nodded significantly. "Such a nice, sweet girl. Everybody likes her, and she likes everybody. Am I right?"

"Wait a second," Samantha said. "Do you mean that Brittany's going to try to convince Tim she's a nice, sweet person like Nikki?"

Kim's ice-blue eyes gleamed. "What makes you think Tim will buy it?" she said to Brittany. "I mean, he *knows* you now. It was different when he first came to River Heights from Chicago. But you've tried to break him and Nikki up too many times now. He knows what a devious person you are."

"I agree," Samantha said fervently.

"Oh, for heaven's sake," Brittany burst out. "Can't I be nice without you guys wondering if it's a trick? You act as if I'm the meanest, most two-faced person in the world!"

Kim and Samantha shrugged. "Maybe not the *world . . .*" Samantha said, her voice trailing off.

"You're supposed to be my best friends!" Brittany said furiously. She jammed the dress she'd been looking at back on the rack. "I have to get home," she said icily.

She turned on her heel and stormed out. Kim and Samantha had a nerve! Well, they'd better apologize the next day. The one time in her life she was sincere, and her friends thought it was all an act.

So what if Tim Cooper was gorgeous and available? So what if she'd been crazy about him since the first moment she saw him? Her transformation was for real. If Tim just happened to notice it, she wasn't going to complain, of course. But Samantha and Kim had better accept that she was a nice, sweet person — or she'd dish up some very nasty revenge!

2 〜〜

The next day at lunch Samantha and Kim saw Brittany pause at the table where Christina Martinez and Mark Giordano were sitting. Mark, the center of the River Heights High football team, had recently asked Chris, the cocaptain of the cheerleading squad, to go steady. The school was buzzing about their romance. Kim and Samantha could hear Brittany's laughter above the cafeteria din.

"She's not going to come over here until we beg her," Kim said, stirring her yogurt vigorously. "She deliberately came to school late so she wouldn't have to see us this morning. She wants an apology. Well, she can just wait forever as far as I'm concerned."

Sighing, Samantha unwrapped her sandwich. "You two drive me crazy," she said in her soft southern drawl. "You're blowing this up into a big deal. Let's just apologize and get it over with. You know we will eventually, anyway."

"Well, I'm not going to be the one to beg her to sit down over here," Kim declared.

"Fine." Samantha put down her sandwich. "Brittany!" she called. "Come on—I saved you a seat!"

Brittany looked over. She hesitated, then said goodbye to Mark and Chris and walked up to her friends' table. "Oh, hi," she said.

"Listen," Samantha said firmly, "Kim and I just wanted to say we were sorry about yesterday. We didn't mean that you were a fake or anything."

Brittany sat down. "I just want my best friends to believe me, that's all," she said.

"Of course we believe you," Samantha said. "Don't we, Kim?"

"Sure," Kim muttered.

Brittany beamed at them. "Thanks, guys." She took an apple from her purse. "So what's new?" she asked, biting into her apple.

"I've been going crazy on this history project," Samantha said gloomily. "It's due a week from Friday. I think Mr. Greene pulled a dirty trick to have a big project due right before Winter Carnival."

"It won't be much of a Winter Carnival

this year, anyway," Kim said. "It's too warm to snow."

"My project is due next Friday, too," Brittany said. "Ms. Marshall is as bad as Mr. Greene."

"What's your topic?" Samantha asked. "Mine's the causes of World War One."

"I don't have a topic yet," Brittany said, taking another bite of her apple.

"You don't? But Brittany, you have less than two weeks left!"

Brittany shrugged. "I'll think of something."

"Are you guys going to Commotion this Friday night?" Kim asked. Obviously she was bored with the topic of Brittany's and Samantha's history projects. "There's supposed to be a dynamite band. Everyone's going."

Commotion was a club for teens that served soft drinks. When a good band played there practically all of River Heights High went.

"I'm definitely going," Brittany said.

Samantha picked at her sandwich. Everyone would be at Commotion Friday night. She was dying to go, but Kyle hadn't asked her yet. Kyle would ask her soon—she was sure. But then she wasn't *positive* he'd ask her. She didn't like that feeling at all.

Over the past couple of days Samantha had

begun to feel just a little uneasy. Other girls were starting to notice Kyle. On one hand, that was good—it meant he was worth going after. But she didn't want anyone to horn in on her territory. She hadn't told the truth to Kim and Brittany at the mall. Lara Bennett *did* worry her a little bit.

Samantha sneaked a look at the back of the cafeteria. She knew the table where Kyle usually sat with the rest of the River Heights High grinds. He was always trying to get her to sit with them. But now his seat was empty.

She scanned the cafeteria quickly. Finally she spied him perched on a windowsill, right next to Sasha Lopez, the flaky but pretty artist. The two of them were talking and laughing.

Samantha felt her heart beat faster. It wasn't as if Sasha was any competition. She was pretty—kind of—but you'd barely notice. She wore black constantly, and her hair, done up in spikes, looked as if she never bothered looking in a mirror. How could a girl ever hope to catch a boy if she never smiled? Sasha was just too intense. Everybody knew you had to be light and easy with a boy. You had to smile and flatter him and laugh at his jokes.

No, Sasha Lopez was no competition, but maybe it was time Samantha staked out her territory just the same. It was time that all of River Heights High knew that Kyle Kirkwood was hers.

Nikki Masters anxiously searched the cafeteria for a place to sit. When she saw Robin Fisher across the room she waved and hurried over with her tray.

"I'm glad I caught you alone," she said to Robin. She sat down next to her friend and leaned closer. "Cal and Niles will be here any minute, and I wanted to talk to you about——"

"Lacey," Robin said, nodding vigorously. The bright orange scarf she had tied in a bow on her head bobbed cheerfully, but her huge dark eyes were worried. "Lacey's always been your basic overachiever," she said. "But she's trying to do too much now. Her job at Platters, her schoolwork, her duties as class secretary, *and* being at Rick's bedside every minute."

"She told me she had only five minutes for lunch today," Nikki said with a sigh. "She has to work on her history project, then try to get out of the junior class officers meeting after school."

Robin nodded sympathetically. "We've got to figure out a way to help her out."

"But how?" Nikki asked. "Do you think we can talk her out of sitting by Rick's bed hour after hour?"

"Hi, guys." Lacey's knapsack hit the table with a thud. "Sorry I can't talk. I have exactly three minutes to eat this tuna sandwich." She sat down, already unwrapping her sandwich, and immediately took a bite. Then she propped open her history book and started studying.

Nikki and Robin exchanged glances. Lacey's fair skin was even paler than usual, and there were dark circles under her light blue eyes. Her red hair was tied back in a loose ponytail, not her usual neat braid. She didn't look like herself.

"What's up, Lacey?" Nikki asked cautiously.

Lacey didn't hear. She frowned at her history book.

"Hey, Lacey!" Robin waved across the table. "Yoo-hoo! Did you notice that your best friends are here?"

"Oh," Lacey said, glancing up distractedly. "Where are Cal and Niles?" Then she immediately lowered her eyes and frowned at her book again.

"They got accepted by an astronaut training program," Robin said. "They're going on the first manned space shot to Pluto."

"That's nice," Lacey said.

"The launch should be any day now," Robin added.

"Great," Lacey said. She turned a page.

Robin rolled her eyes at Nikki. Then she

leaned all the way across the table and shut Lacey's book with a snap.

"Hey!" Lacey exclaimed.

"Your history can wait. Lacey, we're worried about you," Robin said bluntly.

Nikki winced. Robin didn't believe in beating around the bush. "We were wondering how you're doing, Lacey," she said in a softer tone. "You've been so busy since Rick's accident."

Lacey took another bite of her sandwich. "I'm okay," she said, chewing furiously. "I've got all my bases covered."

"Lacey, you're not going to be able to keep up this pace," Nikki said.

"Why not?" Lacey asked stubbornly. She opened her book again.

"Look at you!" Robin exclaimed. "You're a mess. You're not sleeping, you flunked a math test yesterday, and you told me yourself that you might lose your job at Platters because you asked Lenny for this whole week off. Lacey, you can't do everything! You've got to spend less time at the hospital."

Lacey put down her sandwich. "No way," she said. Her eyes were bright, and she was ready to burst into tears. "How can you say that? I *have* to be there when Rick wakes up. I have to be there for him. I can't let him down again!"

"Again?" Nikki asked. Robin's eyes narrowed.

Shakily Lacey began to wrap up the remaining half of her sandwich. "I mean, maybe I should have gone with him that day, that's all."

"But you've never gone rock climbing with Rick," Robin pointed out. "He's never expected you to. You're not exactly the outdoors type."

"So?" Lacey slammed her book shut and stood up. "I can't believe you're doing this," she said in a low tone. "Robin, if it were Cal lying there, you'd be there day and night, and you know it."

"You're right, Lacey," Robin said soberly. "But—"

Nikki shot Robin a warning glance. "Lacey, we just want to help. Tell us what we can do."

Lacey sank back into her chair. She pushed a loose strand of red hair out of her eyes and sighed. "I feel like a bad juggler—all the balls keep dropping. I *am* afraid Lenny's going to fire me. I asked for a leave of absence, and he said I couldn't have it. He'd have to hire someone else—and who's going to take a job temporarily until my boyfriend wakes up? It's hopeless."

Robin sat up. "No, it's not. I'll take the job."

Lacey and Nikki stared at her. "You?" they said together.

"Why not?" Robin demanded. "I've visited you at work a thousand times, Lacey. I know what you do. I can handle it. And I want to help out."

"It's a great idea, Lacey," Nikki said enthusiastically. "That way, you could come back to work whenever Rick is better. You're so close to buying that car! It would be a shame to lose your job."

Lacey nodded. "Okay, I'll ask Lenny. But what about swim practice, Robin? I wouldn't want you to get kicked off the team."

"I'm sure I can work out a schedule," Robin said, waving her hand. "Most of my practices are in the morning, anyway."

Lacey glanced at her watch and stood up. "I have to go to the library. I have a date with Teddy Roosevelt," she said, with a trace of her usual mischievous humor. "Robin, can you come to the mall with me after school?"

"No problem," Robin said.

"Thanks, you guys," Lacey said. "You're the best." Quickly she turned away and walked swiftly out of the cafeteria.

Just then Karen Jacobs scurried past them, following Ben Newhouse. He was stalking across the cafeteria floor so fast no one could keep up. When he finally found an empty table, he set his tray down with a crash and slumped into a chair.

"Ben, you didn't tell me," Karen said as she sat down next to him.

"Tell you what?" Ben asked.

"That you were going out for track," she said impishly. "Are you trying to run a two-minute mile?"

Ben's handsome face broke into a grin. "I'm sorry, Karen. I didn't realize I was going so fast. I'm just so worried about the Winter Carnival."

"It's still almost two weeks away," Karen pointed out. She picked up her fork and dug into her macaroni casserole. She still couldn't get over eating lunch with Ben. It really felt as if they were a couple. They'd only been dating a short time, but Karen was already head over heels in love with Ben.

"Sixty-five degrees," Ben said gloomily. He slammed his cup of soda down in frustration, sloshing the liquid onto the table and into Karen's macaroni. He didn't even notice. "It's like spring outside," he continued glumly.

Karen slid her food slightly away before anything else happened to it. "I know. But I'm sure the warm spell will end soon."

"But when? Do you know what the forecast is for tomorrow? A high of sixty-seven!"

Ben dropped his head into his hands. "I can't stand it. I'm the head of the Winter Carnival committee. If it's a fiasco, it will be all my fault."

Karen put her hand on his arm. "Come on, Ben. We'll think of something."

Ben smiled at her. "I know. I'm glad I have you around to help me." He picked up his sandwich and began to unwrap it.

Karen pushed Ben's books aside so she could reach for the salt. As she pushed his notebook away the edge of a pale pink envelope fell out.

She glanced up at Ben. He was struggling to open the plastic packet of catsup for his french fries. Karen's heart pounded. She shouldn't peek, but she already suspected who the letter was from, and she just had to know for sure. Casually Karen straightened Ben's notebooks. As she did she pulled the pink envelope just a tiny bit farther out in order to read the return address. It said exactly what she'd been afraid of: "Emily Van Patten, New York City."

Ben dipped a french fry into the catsup and grinned at her. Karen smiled back, but she felt like crying. She was being stupid, but she couldn't help it. Emily was off in New York City. Even though he'd been in love with Emily, Ben was dating Karen now. Of course he'd keep in touch with Emily—they were still friends.

All of Karen's old insecurities came rushing back when she thought of Emily Van Patten. Emily was tall, blond, and beautiful, a successful model and actress. Karen just couldn't compete with her. She'd been so thrilled to be dating Ben that she hadn't wondered too much about his old love. Maybe it was time she did.

3

That evening Lacey raced down the stairs and grabbed her coat. "'Bye, Mom," she called as she headed for the front door.

"What?" her mother called from the kitchen. Lacey could hear the sound of something sizzling in a frying pan.

"I'm going to the hospital," Lacey shouted back. She heard footsteps rushing from the kitchen, and she quickly opened the door.

"No, Lacey." Mrs. Dupree's voice was quiet, but it froze Lacey. She had a feeling she wouldn't like what was coming next.

She turned around. Mrs. Dupree was wearing a butcher's apron over her dress-for-success suit. "I want you to eat at home tonight," her mother said.

"But—"

24

"No buts. Come back to the kitchen. My onions are burning."

Lacey trailed back to the kitchen. She couldn't stay for dinner. She just couldn't. She waited until her mother had returned to sautéing the onions and then spoke. "Mom, visiting hours start at seven."

"You were at the hospital after school, weren't you?"

Lacey nodded. "Yes," she said quickly, "but I had to go to the mall first to introduce Robin to Lenny. So I was late getting there."

Mrs. Dupree continued to cook. "Lacey, you can go *after* dinner. I'll drive you so you won't have to take the bus."

"But if I leave right now I can get there right at seven. I can grab a sandwich in the cafeteria. It's a hospital, so they know about good, healthy food." Actually the sandwiches were awful, but Lacey was desperate. She looked for a sign that her mother was weakening, but Mrs. Dupree only took the pan off the burner and turned around to face her.

"Okay," Mrs. Dupree said crisply. "New rule. You will have dinner here every night before you go to the hospital. No arguments." She held up her hand when Lacey began to protest. "Your father and I have hardly seen you since Rick's accident."

Lacey felt like crying. "Mom, I just have to be there."

Mrs. Dupree softened. "I know, honey. But Rick has his family. Don't you think they might want to be alone with him sometimes?"

Lacey paused. She hadn't thought of that. "Mrs. Stratton never said anything—"

"No, she knows how much you want to be there. If you go a little later, Rick's father will have a chance to sit with him. That would give you a little time for yourself, too. Lacey, you can't let everything else slip away."

"I bring my books to the hospital."

"But do you study there?"

"Well, it's hard," Lacey admitted. "But now that Robin is going to cover for me at Platters I can study after school before I visit him. I'll do okay."

Frowning, her mother ran her hand through her short strawberry blond hair. "I remember when 'okay' wasn't good enough for you."

"Mom, don't you see?" Lacey pleaded. "Nothing seems very important now, except Rick."

Mrs. Dupree sighed. "I know, honey. But Rick is going to wake up soon, and then you'll want to spend even more time with him. How can you do that if you have to study because you're failing history or math?"

"But—"

"Lacey," her mother said gently, "I'm not asking you. I'm telling you. You have to eat and get your rest and do your schoolwork and your chores, too. Okay?"

Lacey nodded. "I guess so."

Her mother turned back to the stove. "I'm making spaghetti with sausage just for you. A nice green salad and garlic bread, too. It'll be ready in about a half-hour. Will you set the table, honey?"

"Sure." Listlessly Lacey got out the plates and silverware. Half an hour to wait, fifteen minutes to eat, if she was lucky. She'd have to wait until her parents finished, and they liked to linger over dinner. Lacey felt like screaming. She'd miss a whole hour with Rick!

Maybe if she helped her mother, dinner would get on the table faster. "Mom," she piped up, "can I make the salad for you?"

"That would be great, sweetie," Mrs. Dupree said, smiling.

Hurriedly Lacey gathered the greens from the refrigerator. She felt a little guilty fooling her mother, but she had to be with Rick every moment she possibly could.

* * *

Nikki grinned as Niles Butler finished his fourth piece of pizza. "I thought the English lived on tea and crumpets," she teased. "I can't believe how much pizza you can eat."

"All I have to do is think of that awful English pizza, and I can fit in another slice," Niles said with a grin. "Besides, you know what a fan I am of anything American." His brown eyes were warm as he gave her a meaningful glance.

Nikki blushed and stared down at her nails. She still felt a little awkward around Niles. He said flattering things, but he never made any other moves. The Butlers were only in River Heights for a few months while Niles's father worked with Nikki's grandfather. She'd taken Niles around and shown him all the essentials of being an American teenager: pizza, the mall, the best place to buy records, and driving on the right side of the road.

She'd fallen hard for Niles. He was probably the only boy she knew who could distract her from her confusion about her feelings for Tim Cooper, her old boyfriend. But he kept his distance, and the tension was beginning to get to her.

"I'm glad I could see you on a school night," Niles said.

"I finished my homework right after

school, so my parents said it was okay, but I have to be home by ten."

"No problem," Niles said. "Hey, how do you like that? I used American slang."

"It sure beats 'I shall escort you home at the proper hour, Nicola,'" Nikki said, imitating his English accent.

Niles burst out laughing. His eyes sparkled appreciatively as she laughed along with him. When they stopped Niles was suddenly silent, and Nikki wondered what he was thinking. She wished she could figure him out! She'd had just about enough of that English reserve.

Suddenly he pushed his plate away. "Hadn't we better look in on Robin?" he asked. "If we don't go now, we won't make that movie."

"Right," Nikki said, jumping up. She was glad for the diversion. "I have to admit I can't imagine Robin doing Lacey's job."

"Why not?" Niles asked, amused.

"Well, Lacey's very organized. Robin is— well, you know Robin."

"Let's hope it's a slow night at the record store, then," Niles said.

But as they came up to Platters they could see that the store was mobbed. "Oh, no," Nikki said. "Poor Robin."

They pushed open the glass door and hurried inside. They immediately bumped into Robin, who was rushing toward the stockroom.

"Sorry, guys," she gasped. "Can't talk now."

"Sure," Nikki said, but Robin had already disappeared.

Just then Lenny Lukowski rushed by. He saw Nikki and recognized her. "Where's that friend of yours?" he bellowed. "She messed up another order! Some favor Lacey did me!" Without waiting for a reply he stormed back toward his office.

A few minutes later Robin came out of the stockroom empty-handed and wild-eyed. "Have you seen Lenny?" she whispered.

"He's looking for you," Nikki said. "He's back in his office."

"Good," Robin said. She leaned against a bin of records, nearly toppling them over. "Oh, gosh," she said, steadying them. "I don't know how Lacey does it. You have to keep track of a million things. Listen, thanks for coming by, but I don't have time to talk. Lenny's best customer is up there asking for Evelyn Carter's latest album. I've never even heard of her. Have you?"

Nikki shrugged. "You got me."

"Actually—" Niles said.

"So Lenny says, 'Of course we have it, it just came in, it's in the back room, go get it for the customer, Robin,' with that oily smile of his. So I'm going crazy back there going through the female vocalist stack, and *it's not there.* I'm going to have to bother Lenny again, and he's going to kill me." Robin took a deep breath. "I don't know how Lacey does it, I really don't."

"Robin," Niles tried again, "actually I—"

"Niles, sorry—I have to go find Lenny immediately," Robin interrupted, "so he can kill me."

Robin spun around, but Niles grabbed the tail of her orange shirt. "Wait!" he ordered urgently. "Evelyn Carter is a man. Look under *male* vocalists."

Robin turned back. "A man? Who would name a boy Evelyn?"

"An English mother. He's British."

"Niles, you come from some wild country. And I thought *your* name was weird. But thanks, you're great." Robin dashed back toward the stockroom again.

Nikki and Niles burst out laughing. "You saved the day," Nikki said. "I've never heard of Evelyn Carter. Is he well-known in England?"

"He's becoming rather famous, I suppose," Niles said as they headed for the door. "I heard of him through Gillian. She's the one to talk with about the newest up-and-coming musicians. She was classically trained on the violin, but she loves rock 'n' roll, too."

Nikki was silent as they hurried toward the movie theater. That was the most she'd ever heard about the mysterious Gillian, Niles's girlfriend back in England.

Lost in thought, Nikki followed Niles into the dark theater. She had to admit she felt jealous of Gillian. Had they promised not to see other people while he was in the States? Was that why Niles had never kissed her?

Just then Niles reached over and took her hand. He held it as though it was the most natural thing in the world to do. Happiness coursed through Nikki. He *did* like her!

But what about Gillian? Nikki might have his hand in River Heights, but all the way over in England, did Gillian have his heart?

"This one?" Kyle asked.

"No," Samantha answered flatly.

"I thought maybe this gray shirt—"

Samantha rolled her eyes. "Please." They were in the best men's store in the mall, buying a new shirt for Kyle. Samantha was beginning to wonder if she should bother. Was she dressing Kyle up so he could flirt with Sasha Lopez?

"Here," she said finally. "Try this one, and this one." She shoved two shirts into his arms and added a black cotton sweater.

Kyle frowned. "I think I need to look in some other stores."

"Kyle," she exploded. "We've looked at every piece of clothing in this store. It's the best store."

Kyle looked at her over the pile of clothes. "What's wrong, Sam?"

"Wrong? Why, nothing. Why don't you try on that sweater? I'm sure Sasha will love it. She only wears black." Samantha felt her cheeks flush. How could she be so stupid? Boys hated it when you acted jealous.

Kyle grinned. "Now I see. You're jealous of Sasha."

"No way."

"Maybe if you'd sit with me at lunch once in a while, I wouldn't have to talk to other girls."

"I was talking to Kim and Brittany," Samantha said. As if she'd sit at Kyle's table with all those nerds!

Kyle gave her a sharp look but then shrugged. "Anyway, I heard everyone's going to Commotion Friday night. Do you want to go with me? I thought we could double with Greg and Belinda."

Kyle had to be kidding. Greg Hazen? He probably had a brilliant future as a scientist, but at River Heights High he was strictly a nobody. And Belinda Towser might be a brilliant creative writer, but she had no fashion sense. Greg and Belinda were regulars at Kyle's lunch table full of grinds.

Kyle looked at her quizzically. "Sam?"

She couldn't do it. As much as she wanted to go out with Kyle, she couldn't be seen with his nerdy friends! Samantha tried to stall him. "Friday night?"

"Yes, Samantha. Friday night. It comes right after Thursday." Kyle didn't sound too happy with her.

"Well, that would be just fantastic," she gushed. "I mean going with you. But Kim already asked us to go with her and Jeremy. Do you think we could double with them instead?"

Kyle's brown eyes were puzzled. "You told them we'd double-date with them before I even asked you to go?"

Samantha thought fast. Sometimes Kyle was just too quick for her. "I wouldn't go with anybody else but you."

"That's very noble of you, Sam," Kyle said teasingly. "But do I have to go with Jeremy Pratt? He's such a nerd."

If only Kim could have heard that! Kyle Kirkwood was calling the king of River Heights High a nerd! "He is not," she said loyally. "I mean, I know he can be annoying, but he's not a nerd."

"Samantha, the guy is a jerk and a snob. I

think we'd have a better time with my friends."

Samantha switched into her deepest southern purr. "Oh, Kyle. Now here you are all upset and practically yelling at me just because I want to go to Commotion with my friends."

Kyle sighed. "All right. I'll tell Greg and Belinda we can't go with them."

"Oh, thank you. You'll have fun, I promise." Relief washed over Samantha. She still had Kyle wrapped around her little finger, and she was going to keep him there, no matter what.

4

Brittany saw Kim waiting underneath a tree on the quad Friday morning. Kim was scowling as she scanned the parking lot. "Isn't it a great day?" Brittany said as she strolled up. "Just like spring."

"Right," Kim said irritably. "Have you seen Jeremy?"

"I just got here," she pointed out. "Why? Is he missing?" she asked, trying to sound concerned.

"No, just late. We didn't come to school together this morning, and he was supposed to meet me here." Kim directed her keen blue glance at Brittany. "So what's up with you? Have you snagged Tim for the Winter Carnival Ball yet?"

Now it was Brittany's turn to feel irritable.

She didn't want to have another fight with Kim. "What are you talking about? I'm not after Tim. I told you that a thousand times."

"Riiiight," Kim drawled. "I believe you totally, Brittany."

Samantha came up the walk, smiling at them. "Hi," she said. "Isn't it a beautiful day? I love this warm weather. And I can't wait until tonight to go to Commotion. Kim, I've been meaning to ask you if we could double with you and Jeremy."

Kim looked startled. Brittany knew she was wondering if it would be all right for her and Jeremy to be seen with Kyle, who had been so uncool a short time ago.

"Kim?" Samantha prodded. "Is it okay?"

"I guess so," Kim said slowly. "We couldn't take the Porsche, but—okay, I'll ask Jeremy. *If* he ever shows up."

Brittany frowned. So Kim had a hot date, and Samantha had a hot date—well, at least a date. Meanwhile, her own social life was on the skids.

Just then she caught sight of Tim Cooper. He was standing under a tree all alone, looking even better without Nikki hanging on his arm. Brittany's dark eyes grew thoughtful. When was he going to notice that she was a whole new person?

Across the quad Robin noticed Brittany gazing at Tim. She turned to make sure that

Niles was out of earshot. Cal had taken him over to Mark Giordano for a quick lesson in American football. "Look at Brittany staring at Tim," Robin said to Nikki and Lacey. "She's after him again."

Nikki shrugged. "I'm not surprised. She's never really given up on him."

"Brittany never gives up on anything," Lacey said darkly.

"I just hope he doesn't fall for this new good-girl act of hers," Robin said grumpily. "Everybody's talking about it. All of a sudden she's offering to help people with their homework, or telling them they look fantastic. She came up to me yesterday and told me she liked my outfit. And she wasn't being sarcastic! I thought it was Brittany's twin sister."

Nikki laughed. "I can't imagine why she's turned into such an angel," she said. "Maybe it's just another plot to get Tim. What do you think, Lacey? You're always able to predict what Brittany's motives are."

"I don't know, and I don't care," Lacey said with sudden intensity. "I just know that Brittany Tate isn't someone to be laughed at. She's dangerous."

Nikki looked puzzled. "A pain in the neck, maybe. But dangerous?"

Lacey opened her mouth, then closed it again. She turned to Robin. "How's it going at Platters, Robin? I haven't seen you to ask about it."

Robin and Nikki exchanged a quick glance. They didn't want to worry Lacey any more than she already was.

"Just great!" Robin enthused. "I think it's going to work out. Lenny's really pleased."

Just then Niles and Calvin came up. "We were just talking about how great Robin's doing at Platters," Nikki told them pointedly. She didn't want Niles and Cal to tell Lacey what a fiasco her first day on the job had been.

Quick understanding flashed in Niles's eyes. "Oh, yes, I saw her a couple of nights ago. She was super," he said to Lacey.

Calvin slipped his arm around Robin. "She always is," he said. His green eyes danced. Robin had already filled him in on her troubles at Platters.

"That's a relief," Lacey said. "I was worried. It took me weeks to get the job down. I remember my first few nights were complete fiascoes."

Robin gulped. "You just have to keep your cool, that's all," she said with a bright smile. "It's a cinch!"

Nikki bit back her laughter. She exchanged a glance with Niles, and he winked at her. Then, over Niles's head, she saw Tim watching her. He was standing alone under a tree, and his gray eyes burned into hers. It was almost as though he was *accusing* her of something.

For a moment Nikki felt dizzy. Only a short time ago, if someone had told her that she'd be with another guy while Tim stood across the quad staring at her, she wouldn't have believed it in a million years. It felt so strange, so wrong. Tim should have been over here, laughing with her friends, not staring at her with accusing eyes. The sun went behind a cloud, and Nikki shivered. Suddenly it was as if the whole world had gone crazy.

Then Niles smiled at her, and everything made sense again. He was the boy she was interested in now. Tim Cooper was part of her past. Niles Butler was the person she wanted in her future.

After school that day the *Record* office was crowded. DeeDee had called an emergency meeting, and everyone was buzzing about it. Brittany wondered what the reason could be. She hoped that no one else had come up with a dynamite story. She was still coasting along on her scoop about the cheating scandal, and she didn't want to share the glory. She felt a tiny twinge of guilt that she'd stolen Karen's notes out of her purse in order to get the scoop, but she was sure that Karen never would have written the article.

Just then Brittany saw Karen at the door, saying a very public goodbye to Ben Newhouse. Brittany almost lost her lunch. Did Karen force Ben to walk her to every single function so that every single student at River Heights High would see that they were going out?

She no longer felt bad about scooping Karen—the girl was getting too sure of herself. Brittany had liked her better when she'd faded into the background.

" 'Bye, Ben," Karen trilled. "See you later."

Brittany's eyes narrowed. She'd heard a very interesting rumor that day, and she was dying to let it out at the meeting to see Karen's reaction. Cheryl Worth, one of Emily Van Patten's best friends, had told her that Emily was flying in for the Winter Carnival Ball. But only a mean person would let that piece of information drop. Karen would be devastated if Ben's old girlfriend showed up at the biggest event of the season.

Karen slipped into the seat next to Brittany as DeeDee walked to the front of the room.

"Attention, everyone," she said. "This is

going to be real quick, I promise. I just wanted to introduce you to our new faculty advisor. I think you all know Mr. Greene— he teaches history and social studies to some junior classes and is also in charge of the honors seminar for seniors."

There were a few hand claps, and Mr. Greene stood up. He pushed up his horn-rimmed glasses and stuck his hands in his pockets. "I just want to say that I'm going to step back and let you kids keep doing what you're doing, because I happen to think that the *Record* is a terrific paper."

A couple of kids whistled through their teeth, and Kevin Hoffman, who wrote a humor column, stamped his foot and yelled, "Yo!" Melissa Kravitz, a layout artist, grinned and made a thumbs-up sign.

Mr. Greene held up a hand. "DeeDee is doing a spectacular job as editor. I'm just here to answer questions, be a sounding board. So don't hesitate to call on me." He grinned at all of them.

He seemed nice, Brittany decided, and with DeeDee, he would be the one to choose the editor in chief for next year. Perhaps it was time to get to know him better. Too bad she wasn't in his history class, but wasn't Tim Cooper?

"Thanks, Mr. Greene," DeeDee said,

standing up again. "Now I just want to talk about the next issue for a minute. We're running short—we need one more feature article. Any ideas?"

Brittany thought furiously. This would be an ideal way to impress Mr. Greene. She had to come up with a dynamite idea.

Then Karen piped up. "How about an article on the Winter Carnival, DeeDee? We could play up the fact that the weather has been so springlike, that the committee is tearing its hair out trying to come up with new ideas. It could be funny. And," she added with a grin, "I think I can get the inside story."

DeeDee nodded. "Go for it," she said. "Sounds terrific, Karen."

Brittany felt like screaming. Karen was production editor. Technically, her job wasn't reporting. But time after time she horned in on Brittany's territory.

"So," DeeDee said, "is anything else going on that I should know about? What's new on the social scene, Brittany?"

Great. Now Brittany was just a social columnist while Karen was a features reporter. She almost snapped back something rude to DeeDee, but that wouldn't do her any good. Brittany was furious, and her earlier caution flew out the window.

"Not much," she said idly. "But I did hear that Emily Van Patten might be flying in for Winter Carnival."

Zing! Karen turned pale.

"Let's get a confirmation on that," DeeDee said absently. "Okay, people, that's it."

Brittany felt a tiny bit guilty as she left the meeting. She'd broken her own rule, but she'd slipped up only once. And Karen had deserved it! She was just glad Kim and Samantha hadn't been around to witness it. It would give them more ammunition to distrust her turnaround. It was just so hard to be good all the time. How did other people manage it?

Lacey pushed open the door to Rick's hospital room. Mrs. Stratton was sitting in a chair by his bedside, reading.

"Hi," Lacey said softly. Even though Rick was unconscious, she and Mrs. Stratton always talked in low voices, as if he were sleeping.

Mrs. Stratton smiled. "Hello, Lacey. You're early today."

"I left school a little early," Lacey admitted, slipping into the chair next to her. Then she asked the question she couldn't help asking, even though she knew what the answer would be. Mrs. Stratton always asked it, too. "Any change?"

Mrs. Stratton shook her head. She studied her son. "One day he'll just wake up, Lacey," she said. "I know it."

"I know it, too, Mrs. Stratton," Lacey said. "Oh, I'll be late for evening visiting hours again tonight. My mother makes me eat dinner at home every night." She looked down at her lap. "I'm sorry."

"Oh, Lacey." Mrs. Stratton sighed. "Of course you should eat dinner with your parents. You can't be here every minute."

Lacey looked up. "But I want to be!" she cried.

"I know." Mrs. Stratton reached over and took her hand. "You know, Lacey, I'm glad I've gotten to know you better. Of course, it's a horrible way to get to know your son's girlfriend. But I want to tell you that I think you're terrific."

Lacey couldn't say anything. Mrs. Stratton thought she was a great girlfriend, and Lacey knew she had been the worst ever.

If only she could tell Mrs. Stratton what had really happened, so that she wouldn't compliment Lacey all the time and make her feel so guilty. Lacey couldn't take that chance. If Mrs. Stratton knew about the fight, she would probably kick her out of the hospital.

Just then Rick stirred. He made a noise in his throat, almost a groan, not quite a word. Lacey and Mrs. Stratton both sprang up at the same time.

"Rick!" Mrs. Stratton said urgently. "Rick, it's Mom."

His eyelids flickered, and he moaned.

"Rick? It's Mom. I'm right here. Lacey's here, too."

He opened his eyes for one second. He saw Mrs. Stratton. "Mom?"

"Yes, honey. It's me. I'm right here."

Rick's gaze wavered, then slid toward Lacey. His eyes closed again. In that split second Lacey saw that he didn't recognize her—or didn't want to. Tears sprang to her eyes.

Mrs. Stratton turned to her, her hazel eyes shining. "Oh, Lacey. He recognized me. That's the most alert he's been yet."

Impulsively she drew Lacey into a hug. When she pulled away she smiled through her tears. "Don't cry, honey. He's going to pull out of this! I'm going to get the doctor."

Mrs. Stratton rushed out. Lacey returned to Rick's side. "It's Lacey, Rick," she whispered. "I love you. Please open your eyes again. Please see me. Please."

Rick had slipped back into unconsciousness. Lacey gripped the cold metal of the hospital bed. She knew the worst now. He hadn't recognized her. He had blocked her out of his memory because it was too painful for him to remember the girl who'd betrayed him.

5

On Friday night Samantha waited nervously with Kyle in her driveway. Kim and Jeremy pulled up in Kim's white Mustang only ten minutes late. Jeremy was driving. After he stopped the car he leaned forward to check himself out in the rearview mirror just as Kim tilted it and leaned closer to inspect her lipstick. Their heads collided with a crack.

Kyle snickered as Jeremy scowled at Kim. "Watch it!" he snapped.

"Ow!" Kim rubbed her head, then leaned forward to make sure she hadn't messed up her hair. She collided with Jeremy again.

Kyle burst out laughing. He had a loud laugh, and Jeremy and Kim turned murderous looks on him. They didn't crack a smile.

Jeremy got out and held the front seat

forward so Samantha and Kyle could climb in the back.

"Sorry we're late," Jeremy said, sliding back in the driver's seat. "Kim always is, though."

"Perfection takes time," Kim said coolly.

Kyle rolled his eyes at Samantha. "You look fabulous, Kim," Samantha said quickly, shooting a warning glance at Kyle.

"Nice car, too," Kyle offered.

"It's okay. Too bad we couldn't take the Porsche," Jeremy said. He pulled out of Samantha's driveway and headed toward Commotion.

Kim twisted around in her seat. "So what's new with you, Kyle?" she asked.

"Well, let's see. I've been spending lots of time on my history project," Kyle said. "I'm real excited about it. My subject is the child labor reform movement in the early twentieth century. There's this oral history foundation in Chicago, and I've been going up there on weekends to do research. I've listened to some great tapes. You see, the foundation tapes the reminiscences of people who actually lived through different historical events."

"Fascinating," Kim said in a bored tone.

"Now, my idea of a great tape," Jeremy said, "is the Dead Beats' latest."

Kim laughed and turned back to Kyle.

There was a look in her ice-blue eyes that made Samantha uneasy, the look of a cat playing with a plump, tasty mouse.

"You spend your weekends working on a history project?" Kim asked.

"Well, not *every* weekend," Kyle admitted. He reached over and squeezed Samantha's hand. "I like to spend time with Sam, too."

Samantha squirmed. All of a sudden she wasn't too crazy about Kim knowing that she'd secretly been dating Kyle before his transformation.

"My dad goes up to Chicago a couple times a week," Kyle went on. "He's a history professor at Westmoor, and he's doing research at the oral history foundation, too."

"Sounds fabulous," Jeremy drawled. Samantha saw him exchange a smirk with Kim.

Samantha wanted to stuff her scarf in Kyle's mouth so he'd be quiet. Instead, encouraged by Jeremy, he began to go into the details of his project.

Samantha stifled a groan. He looked so good in his new black sweater, too. Why couldn't he keep his mouth shut and just look cute? Biting her lip, Samantha stared out the window as Kyle droned on. She must have been crazy. Double-dating with Kim and Jeremy was a major mistake.

Samantha was thrilled when she saw the lights of Commotion up ahead. "We're here," she sang out. Thank goodness.

Jeremy found a space right near the front for the Mustang. Commotion was already packed. "It looks like all of River Heights High is here," Kim said in a bored tone as she scanned the crowd. "I knew we should have gone somewhere else. We might as well be in the cafeteria."

"Really," Jeremy said.

"We could go somewhere else if you guys want," Kyle said, his eyes twinkling. He knew very well Kim and Jeremy were exactly where they wanted to be—right in the middle of the action.

"We might as well stay, as long as we're here," Kim said quickly.

Jeremy rubbed his hands together. "What do you say we get some sodas for the girls?" he said. "I'm parched."

"Sure," Kyle agreed.

After the guys left, Samantha waited nervously for Kim to say something about Kyle. She was torn between being irritated at Jeremy and Kim for egging him on, and being embarrassed by Kyle.

"Kyle is a doll," Kim said, her eyes still scanning the crowd. "But doesn't he talk about anything but school?"

Samantha thought fast. Maybe it was better to take the offensive. Tackle Kim and bring her down. "Oh, I just love how smart Kyle is," she gushed. "He really challenges me. It's definitely better than going out with guys who only talk about their cars."

Kim gave her a sidelong glance, trying to decide if Samantha was making a crack about Jeremy. Samantha smiled back innocently, and Kim's mouth shut with a snap.

The tackle had worked! Kim had hit the dirt. Still smiling, Samantha turned back to the band.

Her smile faded when she saw Jeremy across the room heading toward them, balancing three cans of soda. Where was Kyle? Samantha craned her neck to see over the crowd.

Then she saw him with Sasha Lopez by the refreshment stand. The music was loud, and Sasha was leaning close to hear what Kyle was saying. Her hand was resting on his shoulder, and she smiled up at him. Kyle smiled back.

Furious, Samantha pressed her lips together. This had gone way too far! Well, two could play at that game.

"Having fun?" Kim asked her, her eyes on the band.

"Loads," Samantha said, gritting her teeth.

Kim looked at her curiously. "What's the matter?"

Samantha shrugged. "I like Kyle a lot, but it doesn't hurt to check out the action, too." She sighed. "Too bad it's such a dead night."

"You're still looking?" Kim asked.

Samantha smiled. "I'm *always* looking. I'm not going steady, am I? I wouldn't mind dating someone else, too. Got any ideas?"

Kim started to shrug, then stopped. A gleam lit up her blue eyes. "As a matter of fact, I do. How about Tim Cooper? He's *very* available."

Samantha shook her head. "You must be crazy, Kim. What about Brittany?"

"Haven't you heard?" Kim asked innocently, widening her eyes. "Brittany's not after him. So if you went after him, what could she say?" Dropping her innocent pose, she smiled wickedly.

"That's true," Samantha agreed slowly. She was pretty sick of Brittany's holier-than-thou act, too. She wouldn't mind pricking her balloon.

Samantha smiled dreamily. Flirting with Tim might not be a bad idea. She could make Kyle *very* jealous. And if it meant making Brittany squirm, it would be double the fun!

Karen shifted uncomfortably in her chair. She tried to look interested in what Ben was saying. But if he talked about the springlike weather one more time, she was going to stab him with a thermometer.

Well, at least he wasn't thinking about Emily Van Patten, Karen told herself. She was dying to ask Ben if he knew that Emily might fly in for Winter Carnival, but something held her back. She sighed out loud accidentally. Ben's handsome face melted into a grin. "I'm being a jerk, aren't I?" he said.

"Not at all," Karen said quickly. When Ben raised his eyebrows she smiled. "Well, maybe a little bit. Can't you take tonight off?"

"Sure. Tonight I'm just going to think about you, Karen Jacobs." Ben leaned over and kissed her. "Let's dance," he murmured. "A nice slow one."

She smiled. "Now that's more like it," she said.

Ben took her hand and led her to the middle of the dance floor. Just as they reached it the song ended, and the band stopped for a break. Ben grinned. "So much for romance," he said. "What I'd really like," he continued, leading her back to a dark corner, "is to be on a island with you right now. This place is too crowded."

"That sounds wonderful," Karen said breathlessly. Ben had never said such a romantic thing to her before. "I'd like that, too. Which island should we pick?" she asked mischievously. "Barbados? Antigua? Saint Croix? Jamaica?"

Suddenly Ben snapped his fingers. "That's it!"

"What?"

"That's what we'll do for Winter Carnival," Ben said excitedly. "We'll have a *tropical* Winter Carnival."

"What's that?" Karen asked dubiously.

"It's a *theme.* Finally! Every event needs a theme, Karen. We'll all wear Hawaiian shirts and sunglasses. Winter in Barbados!"

"But what about the events?" Karen asked dubiously. "We can't do summer things. Nobody will swim in Moon Lake, and it's too chilly for picnics or softball."

"True." Ben frowned, thinking hard. "But we can't have skating races or snow sculptures, either. We could do other things, funny things. I'm not sure *what* yet, but——"

"I know!" Karen interrupted. "Mixed doubles on the tennis court, but with everyone wearing down vests and mittens."

"That's the idea! And we could have mixed doubles miniature golf in hats and scarves——"

"How about a relay race?" Karen suggested. "Whichever team can get in and out of ski clothes the fastest."

"*Without* their sunglasses falling off," Ben added. "I think it could work! I'd better find Sasha—she's head of the decorations committee. Maybe we should change the theme for the ball, too. Have palm trees instead of snowflakes." Ben hugged her. "You've saved the day, Karen!"

Karen beamed. She didn't mind that Ben had rushed off. She'd helped him save the Winter Carnival!

Niles was a great dancer. Nikki had never danced with him before, but she wasn't surprised that he was so great on the floor. He was elegant in a casual, offhand way. During the slow numbers he held her without any awkwardness. But Nikki found herself wishing he'd hold her just a little closer.

When the band took a break Nikki and Niles collapsed with a happy sigh on one of the platforms ringing the huge dance floor. "Where are Robin and Cal?" Niles asked.

Just then Robin and Calvin came in the door. Robin was wearing a black tuxedo with a white shirt. As they drew closer Nikki saw that the shirt had large multicolored buttons.

"I love your outfit," Nikki called.

"But it's a little, ah, understated for you, isn't it, Robin?" Niles teased.

Robin grinned and raised her pants legs.

She was wearing wildly patterned hot green and pink socks and patent leather oxfords. She did a little jig for them.

"Now I feel better," Niles said solemnly.

They all laughed as Calvin and Robin sank down next to them on the platform. "How did the job go tonight?" Nikki asked.

Robin groaned. "Don't ask. I think I finally figured out the system in the stockroom, but I'm still a menace on the cash register. Today some poor guy bought a Rockability album—and I rang it up at fifty-six dollars! He screamed so loud Lenny came running out from the back room."

"How's Lenny taking it?" Nikki asked, smiling.

Cal clutched his hair with both hands. He widened his eyes. "Robin, Robin, Robin!" he squealed in a good imitation of Lenny's high-pitched voice. "You're driving me out of business, kid!"

Nikki and Niles burst out laughing. Robin stuck her tongue out at Calvin. "Thanks, Roth," she said good-naturedly. She turned back to Nikki and Niles. "I don't know how Lacey does it. I've never heard of half of these groups! What I really need to do is to stash Niles in the stockroom so I can run back and ask for information."

"I'd be happy to oblige," Niles said. "But

it's my friend Gillian who really knows her stuff. She's supposed to come for a visit soon. Maybe I could talk her into it."

"Sure," Robin said airily. "I'll take all the help I can get." But she shot a questioning look at Nikki. This was the first they'd heard about a visit from Niles's old girlfriend.

"Gillian is coming to visit?" Nikki asked Niles in what she hoped was a normal tone.

"She mentioned it," Niles answered. "I'm not sure when, though. I'd like you to meet her, Nikki."

"It sounds like fun," Nikki said. About as much fun as a pit of rattlesnakes.

Robin shot her another look. With her big, expressive dark eyes, Nikki knew what it meant: "We have to talk. Privately."

They'd never have any privacy at Commotion. It would have to be the next morning. "Robin, you have to come over tomorrow," Nikki improvised. "You said you'd help me hem that dress, remember?"

"I remember," Robin said quickly. "I'll come over right after breakfast."

"Wait a second, Robin. You can't sew," Calvin pointed out.

"I'm learning," Robin said through a tight smile.

"But I thought you hated——"

"Let's dance, Cal," Robin interrupted.

Taking his hand, she practically dragged him onto the dance floor.

Niles took Nikki's hand. "Want to try again?"

"Sure." Nikki followed Niles onto the dance floor. She couldn't wait until the next day. She'd have a powwow with Robin and Lacey—that always made her feel better. Lacey would be logical. Robin would be emotional. They would both tell her it was a complete waste of time to worry about an old love. If they told her enough times, Nikki just might believe it.

6

Brittany had to wait until Tim drifted over to drink his soda by himself in a corner. She didn't want Kim or Samantha seeing her talking to him. They'd think she was still trying to get him for herself. Of course, she was—but she didn't want them to find out. If she fixed it right, they'd think Tim was pursuing her.

She'd thought of the scheme the night before. Like all of her best ideas, this one served a double purpose. It would get her not only Tim Cooper, but also the job of editor in chief next year! She'd already worked out the details—now she just needed Tim to swallow the bait.

"Hi, Tim," she called as she came up. "I saw you all by yourself. Don't you like the band?" She leaned against the wall next to him.

"Sure," Tim said. "I just wanted to be by myself for a while."

Brittany could see from this vantage point that Tim had a perfect view of Nikki and Niles dancing. Normally she would have bulldozed ahead and tried to capture Tim's attention. Not now. No matter how hard it was, she was going to show Tim that she'd really changed. Then she'd reel him in.

"Oh, I'm sorry," she said. "I'll leave you alone, then." She pushed off the wall.

"No, wait, Brittany. I didn't mean it like that. You can stick around, please."

Brittany smiled in what she hoped was a shy way. "Well, if you're sure I'm not bothering you." She leaned against the wall again.

Tim shot her a puzzled look. "I've been hearing about your new personality," he said. "What are you up to now?"

Brittany acted hurt. In fact, she *was* hurt. "I really must have been a horrible person," she said around the lump in her throat. "Nobody can believe I have a nice bone in my body."

"You could say that," Tim said.

If it were any other guy, Brittany would have stalked off. Since it was Tim, she just sighed. "Well, I guess I deserved that," she said. "I'll tell you the truth, Tim. It was Rick

Stratton's accident. When something like that happens, it really makes you think. What if that were me, lying in the hospital? If I had to look back on my life, I'd want to see good things, you know?"

Tim nodded. "I know," he said soberly. "Sometimes a tragedy *can* really change you."

Of course. Tim had lost a good friend in a drunk-driving accident. How could she have forgotten that, even for a minute?

"So even though I wasn't close to Rick," she went on, "his accident has really affected me. I'm going to try not to mess up my life anymore."

Tim looked almost convinced. "I hope you mean it, Brittany," he said.

She nodded. "I do." Then she smiled her prettiest, friendliest smile, the one her father called a two-thousand-watter. "But I don't want to bore you. Tell me what's going on with you. How's your history project coming along?"

"Slow," he admitted.

"What's your topic?" There was the key question. She hoped it wasn't *too* boring.

"The muckrakers—you know, the investigative journalists back in the early part of the century. They exposed corruption in government and corporations, investigated factory and slum conditions, stuff like that."

Brittany looked at him, openmouthed. "You're kidding! That's my topic, too!" At least it was as of two seconds ago.

"Really?" Tim asked. "That makes sense for you, doesn't it—since you're a journalist."

"Exactly. I'm concentrating on the women muckrakers." Brittany fervently hoped there *were* women muckrakers.

"I didn't know there were that many. You mean like Ida Tarbell?"

"Exactly. She's the one I'm concentrating on." Whoever she was. "Oh, no wonder I'm having trouble getting the books I need at the library!"

Tim looked puzzled. "But I've done most of my research with articles. I haven't checked out that many books—a couple of reference ones."

Brittany gave her silvery laugh. "That's what I meant," she said. "Every time I looked for a reference book it was out."

"Which reference books are you looking for?" Tim asked.

Brittany hesitated for a second. She wished he'd stop asking her questions about research she hadn't started yet. "I have an idea," she said. "Why don't we compare notes? There's no reason we can't, as long as we don't copy from each other."

Tim nodded. "We could do it tomorrow, if

you want. I'm going to the library in the afternoon."

"Me, too! I could meet you there." Brittany would have a ton of work to do that night and the next morning to prepare. But it would be worth it. She had a date with Tim. Her plan was set in motion.

On Saturday morning Robin and Lacey sprawled across Nikki's bright-colored quilt and discussed the latest burning question— just how "ex" was Nigel's ex-girlfriend Gillian? And how did Niles feel about Nikki?

Lacey was only half listening to the discussion. Of course, she was concerned about Nikki, but it was hard for her to keep her mind on anything but Rick.

"I know they keep in touch," Nikki said, tucking her legs underneath her as she sat on a scatter rug. "But why does she want to come to America?"

"Maybe he doesn't want her to come, and he's just being polite," Robin offered.

Nikki shook her head. "I don't think so. He's not discouraging her. He's looking forward to her visit, he said."

"I don't care what it looks like," Robin said. "I think he's got to be madly in love with you."

Nikki gave a wry smile. "I wouldn't go that far, Robin."

"You could go nuts trying to figure this all out," Robin observed. "I'd say just make the first move. Grab him and kiss him."

Nikki gave a peal of laughter. "I can't do that!" she exclaimed.

"Sure you can. Don't you think she can, Lacey?" Robin asked.

Robin's question seemed to come from miles away. Lacey sat up, shaking her head a little to clear it. "Absolutely," she said firmly. She tried to think back and figure out what she was agreeing to.

Robin clapped her hands together. "Well. Now that we've got that settled, it's time to tackle the next problem. Lacey Dupree."

Lacey sat up. "Me?"

Robin crossed her arms. "We want to know what's going on with you."

"What do you mean?" Lacey asked. "You know what's going on. Rick hasn't regained consciousness since that one time he recognized his mother. Which reminds me, visiting hours start soon, and—"

"You have plenty of time," Nikki broke in firmly. "I promised to drive you to the hospital, remember? But we're not going anywhere until we get to the bottom of this. Something more than Rick being in the hospital is bothering you." Robin stared at Lacey expectantly.

Lacey didn't know what to say. She didn't want to lie to her best friends. But she couldn't tell anybody it was her fault Rick was in the hospital.

So she'd have to tell them something else. "It's my parents," she blurted out. "I'm so mad at them I could scream."

"Why?" Robin and Nikki asked together. They seemed to be relieved that she was finally sharing something with them.

"What did they do?" Robin asked, wide-eyed.

"They're making me eat dinner with them every night!"

"And?" Nikki asked, not believing what she was hearing.

"Well, that's it. It's taking away a half hour, sometimes forty-five minutes, that I could be with Rick!"

"But, Lacey," Nikki pointed out hesitantly, "you go to the hospital every afternoon and every night. If you didn't eat dinner with your parents, they'd never see you."

"I don't blame them for wanting you to eat with them," Robin said bluntly.

Lacey sprang to her feet. Tears filled her eyes, and her cheeks felt flushed. "Whose side are you on, anyway? I don't know why you guys can't support me. You're trying to keep me away from Rick, and I won't let you!" She burst into tears.

Nikki sprang up worriedly. "We didn't mean that! We just think that maybe you're going a little overboard—"

"No, I'm not!" Lacey hurriedly thrust her feet back into her flats. "I'd better go," she said stiffly.

"I'll drive you—"

"No," Lacey broke in. "I just remembered I have to—stop at home first. I'll catch the bus from there." She didn't have to go home at all, but she couldn't bear to be with Robin and Nikki for one second longer.

"Lacey, wait!" Robin called.

"Lacey, come on!" Nikki said.

The door banged shut behind Lacey, drowning out the voices of her friends.

On Monday morning Brittany blew a strand of hair out of her eyes as she juggled her heavy history books. Where were all the boys with crushes on her when she needed them? It was bad enough she'd spent the entire weekend on her history project—now she had to work on it during all her free periods this week, too.

Tim had turned out to have an annoying amount of interest in this project. When they'd met at the library he started right in on work. Brittany had to show Tim she was serious about the project, so she had to be just as dedicated. They worked straight through until closing time without a single break!

At least he hadn't suspected that she had just picked the topic the night before. Brittany had stayed up practically all night Friday, making notes from some books at home. Luckily, her father was a history buff. Then she'd raced to the library early Saturday morning to do more research. The sacrifices she'd made for that boy!

Speaking of that boy, what was he doing with Samantha? Brittany almost dropped her books. What did Samantha think she was doing? She knew Tim was off limits!

Brittany frowned. Samantha could be tough competition — her southern technique was deadly. The honeyed, cooing voice, the flattery, the low, teasing laugh. Could he be tempted by that molasses-and-magnolia act?

Quickly Brittany sped over to the other side of the quad where she saw Kim and Jeremy. When she was close to them she slowed her pace and lifted her hand in a casual wave.

"Hi, guys," she said. "What's new?"

"Not much," Kim said offhandedly. Brittany knew that gleam in those keen blue eyes. Kim must know that Brittany had seen Samantha and Tim together, and she was just waiting for Brittany to explode.

Well, she wouldn't give Kim the satisfaction. She'd die before she mentioned Samantha and Tim. "How was your double date Friday night?" she asked. "I didn't get to talk to you at Commotion."

Jeremy grinned. "Great, if you like being bored to death. All Kyle talked about was his history project for Mr. Greene."

Kim laughed. "He goes up to Chicago every single weekend to some oral history place and listens to these old people talk on tapes."

"About what?" Brittany asked. She was momentarily diverted from her desire to know what was going on with Samantha and Tim. An idea began tickling at the back of her brain, but she couldn't quite get hold of it.

"I don't know and I don't care," Kim said irritably. "But you know, I think Samantha is getting bored with Kyle already."

That gave Brittany her cue. "Where is Samantha?" she asked innocently. "She's usually here by now."

Kim gave a crafty smile. "Oh, she's over there talking to Tim Cooper," she said. "They're right by the big oak tree, Brittany. You can't miss them."

Brittany glanced over her shoulder. Samantha was standing even closer to Tim. Her head was tilted back, and she was smiling up at him through half-closed eyes. A horrible thought occurred to Brittany. What if Samantha got Tim to ask her to the Winter Carnival Ball?

"It's lucky you're not interested in Tim anymore," Kim drawled behind her. "I mean, at first we thought your new image was just another scheme to get him. But you convinced us you were for real. So Samantha figured Tim was fair game."

Brittany fumed. If she showed Kim how furious she was, she'd know her transformation was all an act.

Swallowing hard, Brittany turned back to Kim. "Sure," she said in an offhand way. "I wish her luck."

"You do?"

"Absolutely."

Brittany smiled sweetly. Inside she was plotting a brand-new strategy. She had just come up with a way to get Tim all to herself. Enough Ms. Nice Guy. The real Brittany was back!

7

Brittany darted through the halls to the classroom where Mr. Greene would be just finishing with a senior history class. She waited impatiently for a student to stop talking to him. Then she ran up to him as he packed his briefcase.

"Mr. Greene? Hi. I'm Brittany Tate."

"Ah, yes, of course I know you, Brittany. What can I do for you?"

"Well, I'm in Ms. Marshall's history class. I'm doing a report on women muckrakers for my project, and Tim Cooper is doing a report on muckrakers for you."

"Yes, I know."

"I'm so fascinated with the topic. Tim told me you gave some dynamite lectures—I wish I could have heard them," Brittany said, fixing her dark eyes on Mr. Greene. "Those early reporters did such important work. I think it will help me as a journalist to know more about the history of my profession."

"That's very commendable, Brittany."

"Anyway, I had a brainstorm this morning. I was wondering if Tim and I could combine our projects and do a presentation for both classes."

"It's not a bad idea, Brittany," Mr. Greene said thoughtfully. "Does Tim want to do this, too?"

"It was his idea!" Brittany crossed her fingers. It was only a little lie, and it was a *good* lie. She was giving Tim the credit for her terrific idea, wasn't she?

Mr. Greene nodded. "I'd have to talk to Ms. Marshall first, but I think it will be fine. She's very open to new ideas, I've found." Mr. Greene cleared his throat awkwardly. "So I'll talk to her," he added unnecessarily.

Why did Mr. Greene look so uncomfortable suddenly? He was practically blushing! Just then Brittany had another brainstorm. Mr. Greene must be a bachelor—he wasn't wearing a ring. She knew that Ms. Marshall wasn't married, and she was kind of pretty in a studious way. It couldn't hurt Brittany's chance at becoming editor to give them an opportunity to get together. Mr. Greene just might be grateful to her.

"I thought it was too bad that we don't get a chance to see what the students in other classes have done," Brittany went on.

"I see. You think it might be a good idea to combine both classes for all the presentations," Mr. Greene said thoughtfully.

"Well, it's just an idea," Brittany said.

"It's a good one," Mr. Greene said with a decisive nod. "I'll talk to Ms. Marshall today. Thank you, Brittany. I like your initiative!"

"Thank you," Brittany said modestly. She smiled triumphantly as she hurried to her next class. Bingo! She'd wrapped up Mr. Greene and Tim Cooper in one fell swoop!

After a long morning of classes Lacey ate her lunch in the gym so she wouldn't have to go to the cafeteria. A class of freshmen was playing volleyball, and she had to put up with the players' screams and the shrill whistle of Coach Dixon, but it was better than facing Nikki and Robin. Lacey was still angry with her friends, but she wasn't sure why. All she knew was that she wasn't ready to make up.

As she was crumpling up her sandwich

wrapper and paper bag the gym door creaked open. Lacey steeled herself—she was sure it would be Nikki or Robin, or both. But it was Ellen Ming.

"I've been looking everywhere for you, Lacey," Ellen said as she approached. "This is the last place I decided to look."

"I had some studying to do, and it's quieter here," Lacey said. Just then the freshmen screamed as someone made a good shot. Lacey winced. "I guess I just wanted to be alone," she admitted.

"I'll be quick, then," Ellen said. "I hear you got in trouble with Mrs. Wolinsky."

Lacey sighed. "I'll say. I've missed a few class meetings since Rick's accident, and I left early for the other ones. She thinks that if I can't handle the office, I should give it up. She was nice about it, but she definitely made her point."

"Well, I think I have a solution," Ellen said. She perched on the bench next to Lacey and smoothed out her perfectly pressed pants. Ellen was always neat and crisp. Her silky hair fell in a perfect straight line to her chin. She never seemed to have ink on her fingers or a spot on her blouse. But her brown eyes often twinkled with mischief, and she had a sly sense of humor. Lacey liked her.

"Let me help you out," Ellen went on. "I

can do your job as well as my own temporarily."

"Be class secretary *and* treasurer?" Lacey asked doubtfully. "Isn't that too much?"

"I can handle it," Ellen said. "I already cleared it with Mrs. Wolinsky. I really want to help you, Lacey—we all need help sometimes."

Ellen's petite, pretty face looked strained. Lacey hesitated. "It will take a lot more of your time," she pointed out.

Ellen gave a brief wry smile. "It's okay. I don't mind being out of my house more."

What did that mean? Lacey wondered. But she didn't feel close enough to Ellen to pry. "Well—"

"Please, Lacey," Ellen said. "I feel so bad about Rick. There's nothing I can do for him except help you."

Ellen's soft brown eyes were so concerned that Lacey relented. "Let's give it a try," she said. "But if you start to feel stressed out, you promise to let me know?"

"I promise."

Lacey smiled. "This is really nice of you, Ellen."

"We're all rooting for Rick, Lacey," Ellen said. "I know he'll be up and around real soon."

"I hope so," Lacey said softly.

Ellen stood up to go. "I heard Robin took over for you at Platters," she said.

"Yes."

"And Nikki organized that collection for Rick. That was a really great idea."

"Collection?"

Ellen's hand flew to her mouth. "Oh, no. I blew it. It must be a surprise."

"What collection?" Lacey asked again.

"Well, I might as well tell you. Nikki took it up last week. It's for when Rick wakes up. She thought flowers would be stupid—we couldn't see him surrounded by roses—so we got him a subscription to a sports magazine and a membership in the video club. He gets fifteen free movies! That should keep him from getting bored."

"What a great idea!" Lacey exclaimed. "I'm sure he'll love it."

"Well, I'd better let you study." Ellen hesitated for a minute. "You know, I really envy you, Lacey," she blurted out. "You have such good friends. You and Robin and Nikki are so close."

Lacey didn't know what to say. Of course Ellen had no idea that they weren't even speaking right then. "You have Karen Jacobs," she finally said.

Ellen nodded. "I know. We were starting to get close, but since Ben came along I haven't seen that much of her. You and Robin and Nikki seem to stick together no matter what. That's what I'm talking about."

"Oh," Lacey said. She felt a little embarrassed. "If you ever need someone to talk to, Ellen, I—"

"No, everything's just great with me. Listen, I've got to go. I'll tell Mrs. Wolinsky that you agreed. 'Bye, Lacey." Ellen whirled around and ran to the door. Lacey heard her footsteps pattering down the hall. Deep in thought, Lacey opened her book to study, but she couldn't concentrate.

Ellen was right, Lacey knew. She was lucky to have Nikki and Robin. If she hadn't been so wrapped up in her own troubles, she'd have remembered that.

Samantha spooned up her yogurt-and-fruit salad. She'd much rather have a cheeseburger, but the Winter Carnival Ball was too close, and she wanted to look fabulous. Her new dress had to fit.

Now if she could only line up a partner. Samantha's eyes swept the cafeteria. Where was Kyle? She had no idea if her attempt to make him jealous had worked. He'd had his usual grin for her when he saw her in the hall. Did that mean he wasn't affected at all by her outrageous flirting with Tim Cooper that morning?

Sunk in gloom, Samantha finished her

lunch. She could barely follow Jeremy and Kim's conversation about where to eat after the ball. Everyone was going to the Loft, but Jeremy and Kim wanted to go to the country club.

"It's so much classier," Kim said. "We'll be all dressed up, and I don't want to get greasy pizza all over my good dress. Will you come to the club instead, Samantha?"

"I don't know," Samantha answered. "The Loft is casual, sure, but at least it's lively. Everyone at the club seems like they're embalmed." Actually, Kyle had said that after she'd taken him to lunch there once.

Kim arched an eyebrow. "Since when have you turned against the club? People there are more sophisticated, that's all."

Samantha grimaced. "Then go there," she said impatiently. "I'm sure you'll have a great time by yourselves."

"I bet Brittany will want to go," Kim said as though Samantha hadn't said anything. "Since Jeremy and I sponsored her for membership she hasn't been there much at all. I wonder who she's trying to get for her escort to the dance. By the looks of things, it just might be Kyle Kirkwood."

"What?" Samantha exclaimed.

Kim smirked. "Look over there by the soda machine, Sam. Brittany must be trying to get you back for flirting with Tim this morning. So much for her goody-goody act.''

Samantha twisted around in her seat. Sure enough, Brittany had cornered Kyle by the soda machine.

"Looks like a battle shaping up," Kim said. "I'd watch my step if I were you, Sam."

Samantha frowned. Maybe she'd been wrong to flirt with Tim. She didn't want Brittany as a rival. Brittany was just too smart—and devious.

She saw Brittany give one last melting smile to Kyle and then walk over to Tim across the cafeteria. Terrific, Samantha thought hopelessly. Now Brittany was going to capture both of them! She'd give anything to hear what Brittany was saying right then.

Samantha might have been bored if she could hear Brittany's conversation. Brittany wasn't charming Tim at all—she was all business. That was the only way to snag him, she'd decided.

"I hope you don't mind my going to Mr. Greene before I talked to you," Brittany said to him. "But I wanted to clear it with him first. He thinks it's a fabulous idea! In fact, now he wants everyone to give a presentation to both classes. So what do you say? Do you want to do a presentation together?''

"I guess so," Tim said slowly. "Mr. Greene really liked the idea?''

"He loved it!" Brittany said. "With both of us doing research we can really go into the topic in depth. How can we lose? We'll get A's for sure!"

Tim thought for a moment. "You know, it is a good idea," he said finally.

"Do you really think so, Tim?" Brittany asked.

He nodded decisively. "Yeah, I do."

"Good. Because that's not all. I have another idea."

Tim grinned. "You never quit, do you, Brittany?"

She hoped that was a compliment. Brittany decided to take it as one. She grinned back. "No, I don't. You can always make a good idea better. I was just talking to Kyle Kirkwood." She flipped her dark hair over her shoulder and leaned closer to him. "Did you know there is an oral history foundation in Chicago?"

"No," Tim said, shaking his head. "I'm not even sure I know what it is."

"Kyle told me all about it," Brittany said breathlessly. "It's this place that puts people's stories on tape, in their own words. For example, they have some early Chicago politicians talking about political corruption. And people who worked in factories when they were young talking about their experiences. Kyle says they have amazing stuff. He's working on early labor organizers, but he says they have a lot of tapes of muckraking journalists in Chicago! The actual people, Tim. Can you imagine?"

"That sounds great," Tim said, sitting up with new interest. "I'd love to hear some of those tapes. And it would really add something to our project—I know Mr. Greene would go for it."

"I can't wait to hear the tapes," Brittany said. It would be a terrible bore, but with Tim next to her she might be able to stand it.

"The only problem is time," Tim said, frowning. "The presentation is Friday. How could we get to Chicago before then?"

"I was thinking about that," Brittany said. "Maybe since it's a school project we could get out early. And our parents would probably let us go to Chicago, if it's for school."

"Maybe," Tim said. "So would you want to go with me?"

Would she! "I'd love to hear those journalists talking about what it was like to visit tenements and sweatshops." And she'd love to have Tim alone in a car for the trip there and back.

"Okay, let's see what our parents and the school say," Tim decided. "Maybe I could get my mother's car that afternoon."

"Really? Oh, Tim, that would be terrific. Thanks."

Brittany's dark eyes glowed. Her plan had worked like a charm. Sometimes a little scheming was the best way to handle things. She'd decided that honesty only got you so far.

8

After school that day Nikki had an assignment for the *Record*. Karen had submitted her article on the new plans for the Winter Carnival activities, and DeeDee had asked Nikki to take photographs for it.

Nikki was glad when Niles volunteered to be her assistant.

Their last stop was the art room, where Sasha was cutting out a stencil of a huge palm tree and shouting instructions to the rest of the artists, who were fashioning paper leis. The room was in chaos, and Nikki and Niles quickly went to work capturing it. Within a few minutes they had all the pictures they needed.

"I think that's it," Nikki said, putting

on her lens cap. "I can give you a ride home, Niles. Thanks for helping me out today."

"It was fun," Niles said. "I'll take any excuse to spend time with you, Nikki."

Nikki bent over to pack her camera back into the case. She let her blond hair swing forward to hide the blush on her face. She almost wished Niles would stop saying things like that. Now she would spend the rest of the afternoon wondering if he really meant it.

"I was wondering if you'd go to the dance with me, Nikki," Niles said in the hall.

Finally! "I'd love to, Niles," Nikki said warmly.

"Fantastic!" Niles said. He took her hand and held it all the way down the stairs and out into the parking lot.

Now was the perfect time to ask him about Gillian, Nikki thought nervously. But Niles had only asked her to a dance. He had only held her hand. Did that give her the right to ask him about another girl? No, she decided.

"Well," she said brightly, "I guess we can go."

"Right," Niles said, but he hesitated. He was staring down at her with his deep, dark eyes and serious expression. Nikki's heart began to beat faster.

Suddenly Nile reached out and grabbed her arms. Then he pulled her to him and kissed her, right in the middle of the River Heights High parking lot!

Nikki was surprised, but not too surprised to return the kiss. His lips felt firm and very warm. Her heart pounded, and she felt a little dizzy when he pulled away.

"I've wanted to do that for some time," Niles said. He slid his hands down her arms to hold both her hands.

"You have?" Nikki asked breathlessly.

"Oh, yes." Niles looked uncertain. "I like you so much, Nikki," he said slowly. "And I'm going back to England in a few months. I have a whole life back there. Maybe I should say that I like you *too* much. You know what I mean?"

"Gillian," Nikki blurted out.

He nodded. "I've already told you about her. What I haven't told you was that Gillian wrote me a letter last week. She thinks we should see other people, that we're too young to be tied down to each other. I was upset at first. But I think she's right."

"Oh," Nikki said. She gathered her courage and asked, "What does that mean for us, Niles?"

"I don't know," Niles said. "What about Tim Cooper?"

Nikki gulped. "Tim?"

"What does *he* mean for us?" Niles asked. He smiled wryly. "I'm not blind. I see the way he looks at you. And I know how close the two of you were."

"We were close," Nikki admitted, "but things have changed. We didn't know how we felt anymore, so we decided to see other people."

"Exactly like me and Gillian," Niles said. "And you and I are both a little afraid to get involved again. Maybe we're too afraid."

"Maybe," Nikki whispered.

"Do you think that you and I could see each other without anybody getting hurt? You or me or Tim or Gillian?"

"I don't know," Nikki said honestly.

"I've been thinking about that and you from the first minute I saw you," Niles said. "I guess I felt relieved when I got Gillian's letter. She's probably met someone else, too. I'm just glad I could finally kiss you without feeling guilty. I couldn't wait much longer."

Nikki smiled. "I'm glad you couldn't."

Niles slipped his arms around her. "If we take it slow, things could work out."

"Right," Nikki said.

There was a mischievous gleam in Niles's dark eyes. "But before we start to take things slow . . ." he murmured. He bent his head and kissed her again.

Nikki's eyes closed, and she forgot she was in a very unromantic parking lot. All she could feel were Niles's lips and his arms around her. Maybe it couldn't work out. Maybe somebody would get hurt, and maybe it would be Nikki. But right then she just didn't care.

As Brittany took the pan of brownies out of the oven she burned her thumb. "Ow!" she screamed. She danced across the kitchen and thrust her finger under the cold-water faucet. Ten thirteen-year-old girls squealed and laughed.

"Your sister is a riot, Tamara," a freckle-faced blond girl named Mindy said.

Brittany let the cool water rush over her throbbing thumb. This nice-girl transformation was a major mistake. Why had she ever volunteered to chaperon Tamara's after-school party? She must have been crazy!

It was one thing to be nice and helpful at school. She didn't have to drag the act home with her. But a couple of days ago it had seemed like a good idea. When she'd offered, her mother had been very impressed with Brittany's maturity. Even Tamara had been nice to her ever since. Brittany wanted to strangle the kid now. Her friends were a noisy, silly bunch of brats. But a couple of those brats had older brothers and sisters at River Heights High, and they might mention what a fantastic older sister Tamara had.

She shut off the water and turned around.

"How about some ice cream for those brown-ies?" she asked sweetly.

"All *right!*" the girls shouted.

Brittany went to the refrigerator to get the ice cream. As she dished it into bowls she wondered what diversion she could come up with to get the little dweebs out of her hair. She was dying to call Tim to tell him the school had given them permission to leave early on Wednesday.

Brittany had asked Mr. Greene and Ms. Marshall to go to the principal, Mr. Meacham, on behalf of her and Tim. The plan had worked beautifully. Not only did they get permission, but Mr. Greene had been all smiles and chuckles at being near Ms. Marshall. He was kind of cute when he was in love.

While Tamara's friends spooned up ice cream and made stupid jokes Brittany planned the outfit she'd wear on Wednesday. Definitely a miniskirt to show off her legs. But it might be too warm for her boots. She had just decided on her black suede flats when Tamara's spoon clattered into her empty bowl.

"What should we do now?" she asked Brittany.

"Yeah, Brittany. What should we do now?" Tamara's friend Crystal asked. She gazed at Brittany with big blue eyes.

Brittany thought fast. "Why don't you listen to tapes and dance? You can practice for all the boys."

The girls all giggled. "That's a great idea," Crystal said.

"Can we listen to your tapes, Brittany?" Tamara asked.

Brittany's smile grew strained. Her tape player was in her room, and she wasn't crazy about having the kids in there. But she wanted to talk to Tim. "Sure," she said. "If you guys promise to be careful."

"We will," Tamara said fervently.

"Will you show us some new dances, Brittany?" Crystal asked.

What a pest! "Okay. I'll be in in a few minutes," Brittany promised. She waited until all the girls had run into her room, then reached for the phone. She had memorized Tim's number.

Tim picked up the phone on the second ring. "Hello?"

"Hi, Tim. It's Brittany. I have some *very* good news. Mr. Meacham gave us permission to leave early on Wednesday! And my mom said okay, too."

"That's good," Tim said. "My mother said we could take her car."

"Fabulous! I can't wait," Brittany said.

"Me, too," Tim said. "I could use a good grade on this project."

Rats! Brittany frowned. Tim didn't seem the least bit thrilled at having her all alone for the ride to Chicago and back. When was that boy going to wake up and see how terrific she was? She searched frantically for a topic to keep Tim on the phone. She was running out of things to say about the muckrakers.

"Well, if that's all, Brittany, I'd better go. I'm in the middle of studying for a test tomorrow."

"I have to go, too," Brittany said quickly. "I'm chaperoning a party for my little sister."

Tim sounded surprised. "That's nice of you, Brittany."

"Don't let the shock give you a heart attack, Tim," Brittany said lightly.

Tim laughed. "I'm sorry. Listen, have a good time. And I'll see you tomorrow, okay?"

Was that actually a bit of warmth creeping into Tim's tone? Brittany smiled as she said goodbye. She might just be making some headway.

The smile stayed on her face as she walked down the hall to her bedroom. The new Rockability tape was blasting, and she heard excited laughter and chatter coming from her half-open door.

Brittany pushed the door open all the way.

The first thing she saw was Tamara leaning close to Brittany's makeup mirror. Every single lipstick Brittany owned was either lying on the mirrored vanity top or clutched in greedy fingers. Crumpled tissues with smears of pink and mauve and red were strewn everywhere. Next to Tamara was Crystal, with another lipstick in her hand. Another girl was carefully applying Brittany's brand-new blush. A third was trying out some bronze eye shadow. All the girls were crowding around the mirror, trying to get a good look at themselves.

Tamara glanced over at her guiltily. She tried to smile. Her teeth were smeared with pink lipstick.

"You said I could try on your makeup whenever I wanted," she reminded Brittany. "Remember? So I thought it would be okay if my friends did, too."

Brittany had made the offer right after Rick's accident, in a burst of sisterly feeling. She knew she shouldn't lose her temper. She knew these greedy little girls would spread stories about her at dinner tables all across River Heights. She started to count to ten. She made it to two.

"If you brats don't get out of this room in one second, you're all dead meat!" she screamed.

* * *

"So how about that ice cream you wanted?" Kyle asked.

Samantha shrugged. "Sure. Let's go."

"Great." Kyle turned the ignition, and his van roared to life. "Should we try the mall or stay in the neighborhood?"

Samantha looked out the window at the dark night. "Whatever."

"Samantha," Kyle said in exasperation, "you're the one who said you really wanted to go out for ice cream tonight. I left my French homework, I filled my mom's van with gas, and you act like I murdered your cat. Did you want to see me tonight so you could ignore me?" He ran his hand through his dark blond hair. "You're driving me crazy. What's wrong?"

"Nothing," Samantha said. Everything was wrong. She'd flirted with Tim Cooper after school again that day. She'd risked Brittany's wrath. Kyle had seen her, she knew it! So why wasn't he angry at *her*?

"Okay. Fine." Kyle stepped on the gas and roared out of Samantha's driveway.

She opened her mouth to tell him to slow down, then closed it with a snap. She wouldn't give him the satisfaction. She was getting angrier by the minute. She wanted to see him so that he could apologize for flirting with Brittany and Sasha and practically every other girl at River Heights High. She was ready to forgive him. Why wasn't he asking her what was wrong, cajoling it out of her? Why wasn't he jealous of her and Tim?

Obviously he just didn't care about her anymore. Samantha sniffed and stared out into the dark night. She couldn't believe what a mean, insensitive person Kyle was.

Kyle drove to a neighborhood ice-cream parlor, even though he should have known that she preferred the mall. He executed a perfect parallel parking job. "Here we are," he said.

Samantha didn't budge. "I can't believe you brought me here," she burst out. "Don't you care where I want to go?"

"I asked you," Kyle pointed out. "You told me to choose."

"So you deliberately came here, when you knew I wanted to go to the mall! What's wrong with you, Kyle Kirkwood?"

Kyle let out a long breath. "There's nothing wrong with me," he said calmly. "But I can tell you exactly what's wrong with you, Samantha Daley."

"Oh?" Samantha snapped. "And just what is that?"

"You're a spoiled brat," Kyle continued in the same maddeningly calm tone.

"W-what?" Samantha sputtered. "How dare you talk to me that way!"

Kyle twisted around in his seat to face her.

"Ever since we started dating you've treated me like a puppet. First we have to sneak around, with you in those stupid disguises. Now you're trying to get me to be friends with people like Jeremy Pratt. And you want me to ignore my old friends."

"I don't know what you're talking about!" Samantha said angrily. "You're not making any sense at all."

"I don't care how nerdy you think I am," Kyle went on. "I'm not going to drop my old friends. You can change my wardrobe, Samantha, but you can't change *me.*"

"Oh, Kyle, now don't be silly. I don't want to change you. I don't want you to drop all your old friends. I told you that Kim wanted us to double with her and Jeremy."

Kyle held up his hand. "Don't," he said in a serious tone. "Don't lie to me. Jeremy already told me that *you're* the one who asked them to double. And you asked them on Friday morning, *after* I asked you to go with Greg and Belinda. So just decide. Right here, right now. Are you going to keep trying to change me, or are you going to accept me as I am? The first step would be to go out with my friends once in a while."

There was a hard gleam in Kyle's normally soft brown eyes. He wasn't kidding. Samantha hesitated. She wanted Kyle. But she didn't want his nerdy friends, too!

Kyle turned away. He stared out through the windshield. "I thought you were different, Sam. Special. Maybe I was wrong."

"Maybe you were!" Samantha snapped. "Maybe *I* was wrong, too!" She opened the car door. "I thought you were special, too. But you're just another boy ordering me around. Well, I won't listen to your orders, Kyle, and I won't sit here for one more second." Samantha slid out of the car.

"Samantha, wait—at least let me drive you home!"

"I can walk, thank you." Samantha slung her purse over her shoulder angrily. She began to walk away. She listened carefully for the sound of Kyle's door opening, of his footsteps running after her. She even slowed her pace a little bit.

But Kyle didn't come running after her. By the time she reached the corner she'd heard his car start up and drive slowly away.

9

That evening Lacey took the bus to the mall after leaving the hospital early. She'd wanted to talk to Robin and Nikki after school that day, but her English teacher had made her stay after class to talk about her dismal showing on a quiz the week before.

She slipped inside Platters as Robin was ringing up the last customer's sale. Robin didn't notice Lacey as she concentrated on entering the codes into the computerized system.

"That tape is on sale," the customer suddenly said.

Robin looked up. "It is?"

"See? Right here—read the sticker."

"Right." Robin frowned and looked at the

cash register again. "On sale," she muttered. "Just my luck."

Lenny stuck his head out of the office. Lacey ducked behind a display quickly. She recognized his expression. He was close to exploding, but he couldn't do it in front of the customer.

"Robin?" he called out in a syrupy tone that didn't fool anyone. "Having trouble again?"

"No, Lenny!" Robin said gaily. "Everything is under control!" She smiled winningly at the customer.

With a grunt Lenny retreated into his office. Lacey grinned and darted forward. She slipped behind the counter and took the tape from Robin's hand.

Quickly Lacey rang up the sale, put the tape in a bag, and gave the customer his change. When he had left the store, she turned to Robin.

"Okay, Fisher, out with it," she said sternly. "How are you doing at this job for real?"

Robin slumped against the counter. "Terrible," she moaned. "I'm the worst employee in history. Lenny's ready to kill me. If he wasn't so desperate to have you back, he would have fired me the first night. He's just hoping you'll be back soon."

"Why didn't you tell me?" Lacey asked.

"Because I didn't want you to worry," Robin said. "You have enough on your mind."

"Oh, Robin. You're such a good friend," Lacey said with a sigh. "And I'm such an awful one."

"No, you're not! You're the best!"

"I'm sorry about the other day. I want to explain everything to you and Nikki."

"Well, she's going to pick me up tonight," Robin said. "Why don't you stick around and have ice cream with us?"

"Sounds great," Lacey agreed. "Let me help you clear the register before Lenny gets back."

Lacey accomplished the last tasks of the shift in half the time Robin usually took. Then she waited outside while Robin said good night to Lenny. After Nikki joined them they ordered cones and perched on the edge of the fountain to eat them.

Lacey started hesitantly. "When you asked me Saturday morning what was wrong, I felt like I couldn't tell you," she said. "I was too embarrassed, too scared."

"Scared?" Nikki asked.

Lacey let out a long breath. "I'm the reason Rick is in the hospital."

Nikki and Robin both stopped eating and looked at her. "What?" Robin said.

"We had a fight that day," Lacey went on.

"I asked Rick if he was involved in the cheating scandal. Remember that Rick Sutton was one of the boys that got caught? Brittany knew that a 'Rick S.' was going to get in trouble, so she hinted to me that it could be *my* Rick. So I accused him, just like that! He got angry and drove away really fast." Ice cream was slowly melting down Lacey's arm. She wiped it off with her napkin. "He went climbing that night because he was upset. It's all my fault he fell."

Nikki sighed. "It's not your fault Rick slipped, Lacey," she said firmly.

"You're not responsible," Robin chimed in fiercely. "Of *course* you'd ask Rick if the rumor was true."

"I wish I could believe you," Lacey said. "I sit by his bedside every day, feeling awful. It's even worse when his family's there. Especially Rick's mother. She's so nice to me. If she knew the truth, she'd probably kick me out of the room."

Robin frowned and licked her cone. "Lacey, I think you should tell Mrs. Stratton about the fight with Rick."

"What? I couldn't do that!"

Nikki nodded in agreement. "I think Robin is right, Lacey. It's the only way you'll get over the guilt. Mrs. Stratton will understand. She won't blame you."

"I don't know," Lacey said gloomily, "but I'll think about it."

"And meanwhile," Robin said, "what's all this about not going to the Winter Carnival Ball?"

"I can't leave Rick," Lacey said. Her pale blue eyes looked bleak. "How can I dance when he's lying in a hospital bed?"

"You don't have to dance," Nikki pointed out. "But as class secretary, you should be there. You can help with the punch or something. They really need volunteers."

"Maybe you're right," Lacey said, looking as though she was about to burst into tears. Lacey got up quickly to throw away her cone and get some more napkins.

"Lacey thinks Rick's accident is her fault," Nikki said sadly. "What can we do, Robin? Robin?"

Robin was lost in thought. She was staring down at the floor. "She's not going to get away with it," she muttered.

"Who's not going to get away with what?" Nikki asked.

"The rat who repeated that awful rumor to Lacey," Robin murmured. She raised her head. Her dark eyes sparked with anger. "That sweet, helpful Brittany Tate!"

On Tuesday morning Karen barely listened to her chemistry teacher. She was daydreaming about Ben—as usual. They'd talked on the phone for an hour the night before. When Mrs. Melado finished giving the instructions for their lab she realized she had no idea what they were supposed to do. At least she had Ellen Ming for a lab partner. Ellen always paid attention.

"Ellen," she whispered. "What's the first step?"

Ellen's dark eyes looked cloudy. "I wasn't really listening," she admitted. "What's the experiment?"

Karen giggled. "I wasn't listening, either. Let's try to figure it out from the textbook."

Together she and Ellen bent over their book and managed to figure out the first few steps.

"How are things going with you and Ben?" Ellen asked.

"Great," Karen said. "We're both really wrapped up in the carnival, though. We hardly talk about anything else. We're having a bowling party Friday night instead of a skating party at Moon Lake."

Ellen made a face. "I heard. It doesn't sound like it'll be as much fun."

"Oh, I think it will be," Karen said encouragingly. "Ben thought up this fifties retro theme. He got the bowling alley to agree to play old music all night. We're all supposed to wear fifties outfits. I got a poodle skirt from my mom. And there's going to be a dance contest."

"That sounds like fun," Ellen said. "You ought to publicize that more. I hadn't heard that part."

"The committee is putting up fliers today." Carefully Karen mixed two chemicals together in a glass flask.

"Hey, I hear that Emily Van Patten is coming to the ball Saturday night," Ellen said as she bent back over her textbook.

Karen's hand jerked, and one of the chemicals spilled all over the lab desk. She jumped back and knocked over her stool.

Mrs. Melado looked up from counseling another student. "Karen! Be careful. You're lucky that wasn't hydrochloric acid."

"I'm sorry, Mrs. Melado." Karen quickly wiped up the solution.

"*I'm* sorry," Ellen whispered. "I thought things with you and Ben were great. Are you upset that Emily's coming home?" Behind the plastic goggles Ellen's soft brown eyes were filled with concern.

Karen slumped back onto her stool. "What do you mean?" she asked. "Why should I be upset that Ben's ex-girlfriend—the blond, beautiful, famous model he was in love with —is coming back to town?"

Ellen laughed, then quickly stopped when Mrs. Melado shot them a warning look. She bent over her glass beaker. "Try not to worry," she advised in a low tone. "Ben is crazy about *you* now."

"Oh, Ellen, I don't know." Karen sighed. "I think I might care for Ben more than he does for me. We haven't been dating that long, and he was in love with Emily. Maybe he still is."

Ellen thought for a minute. Then she nodded her head decisively. "I'll tell you what I'd do, Karen. I'd ask Ben flat out how he feels. Find out if he still cares for Emily. I think Ben would tell you the truth." Ellen stared off into the distance. "There's nothing worse than secrets," she said.

"But what if he *is* in love with her still?"

Ellen shrugged. "Then you'll know. And you won't be any worse off. Keep in mind that she still lives in New York. You've got time on your side, kiddo."

"That's true," Karen admitted.

Mrs. Melado walked over to their lab desk. "Perhaps you girls could try to catch up to the rest of the class. We're all on step ten."

"Yes, Mrs. Melado," Ellen said. She crossed her eyes at Karen when Mrs. Melado turned away.

Karen felt a little bad. She was always talking about herself with her friends these days. Teresa D'Amato and Ellen were great, giving her advice and listening to her worries, but when was the last time she'd asked about them?

Ellen ran out of the lab as soon as the bell rang. Karen closed her lab book. She had no idea what was going on in Ellen's life, if she had a date for Winter Carnival, or how juggling two class offices was going.

"Some friend I am," Karen murmured to herself as she packed up her books. Maybe it *was* time to ask Ben straight out about Emily. If Karen didn't do it soon, she might lose every friend she had.

All day Tuesday at school Samantha told herself she was better off without Kyle. He had turned out to be a horrible person. So why did she miss him so much?

When the last bell rang she walked out of school in a daze. All she'd thought about all day was Kyle. She kept waiting for him to apologize. She'd planned her reaction, too. She'd gaze up at him from under her eyelashes.

But Kyle had avoided her all day. He was never going to apologize, she knew. And now she didn't have a date for the Winter Carnival Ball!

Samantha was so busy concentrating on her misery that she nearly ran into the muscle-bound Mark Giordano.

"Whoa," Mark said, reaching out to steady

her with one hand. "Something on your mind, Samantha? You almost ran me down."

Samantha blinked up at him. Mark was cute. He was a football star. They'd gone out on a few dates ages ago, but Samantha had quickly grown bored with Mark's endless recitals of touchdowns and completed passes. He and Chris Martinez had been the perfect match. But she'd heard from Kim earlier that day that Mark and Chris had broken up.

"Are you okay, Sam?" Mark asked.

Mark was boring, but he was cute—and available. He might be her last chance for a date to the dance. And wouldn't Kyle be jealous! Mark was everything he wasn't— muscular, athletic, popular.

"Aren't you sweet to ask," she cooed at him. "When you must be all upset yourself today. About Chris, I mean. I heard you guys broke up."

Mark ducked his head. "Nah. I mean, it's probably better."

"But still, it must hurt," Samantha said with wide eyes. "Chris doesn't know what she's missing, Mark."

"Thanks, Samantha. That's nice. I guess I am pretty upset about it." Mark nodded several times, embarrassed. "The thing is, now I have to find someone to enter the tennis match on Saturday with me."

"Well, what about me?" Samantha asked.

"You play tennis?" Mark asked hopefully.

She shrugged. "Sure. I'm not the greatest, but I can get the ball over the net. Besides," she added softly, "you can carry the game for both of us, I'll bet."

"Well, great! You saved my life, Samantha. Thanks."

"Don't you mention it," Samantha purred. She smiled sweetly at Mark and began to count. Any second now he should ask her to the dance. One, two—

Mark cleared his throat. "Uh, Sam? I know it's late notice, and you probably have a date and everything, but I'd like to take you to the Winter Carnival Ball if you're free."

Samantha gave him a dazzling smile. "Why, Mark. What a surprise. I'd love to go to the ball with you. That sounds just perfect!"

10

Brittany had been waiting for days for the trip to Chicago with Tim. She'd fantasized about its every possibility, but never in her fantasies had the possibility of failure occurred to her. She had assumed Tim would have to ask her to the Winter Carnival Ball.

But as she drove back to River Heights with him she had to admit to herself that she'd failed. The afternoon had been a total disappointment.

The oral history foundation hadn't been disappointing, though. She had thought it would be a dusty, ivy-covered building, but it was high-tech, with gleaming stainless steel shelves and modern desks and lights. She and Tim listened to tapes on the most modern equipment. They were even allowed to duplicate parts of the tapes to use in their presentation. Brittany had been surprised at how fast the afternoon passed.

Tim had suggested a hamburger after they were finished, and Brittany tried to convince herself it was a date. It wasn't. Tim treated her only like a fellow student, not as a girlfriend.

Now they were twenty minutes from home, and Brittany was tied up in knots. If she brought up the Winter Carnival Ball, Tim might suspect she was angling for an invitation. But she had to line Tim up before she got out of his car. If she didn't, Brittany Tate wouldn't have a date to the biggest dance of the season! She'd put all her eggs in one basket, and they were going to end up all over her face.

Finally, as Tim took the exit off the highway for River Heights, she gave up. "I'm glad we'll be giving the presentation on Friday," she said. "That way we can enjoy Winter Carnival with a clear conscience."

"You said it," Tim agreed. "I've been working on this project every weekend for a while now. I'm ready to have some fun."

Brittany waited expectantly, but Tim only concentrated on his driving.

Tim's car purred to a stop in her driveway. He grinned at her. "It's been fun, Brittany," he said. "Thanks again."

"Anytime," she said brightly. She reached for the door handle. Tim cleared his throat as if he was about to say something, and she stopped, her heart beating.

Tim twisted around in his seat to face her. Moonlight glinted on his bright gray eyes, and Brittany found herself melting. He was so gorgeous. "Since we were a good team today, maybe we should try dancing at the Winter Carnival Ball together," he said. "Do you want to go with me?"

Brittany almost fell out of the car. He had asked her—just like that!

"I-I'd love to," she stammered.

"Great." Now Tim seemed a little uncomfortable, as if he was surprised that he had asked her.

Brittany decided she should get out of the car quickly in case he changed his mind. "Good night, Tim. Thanks for driving today."

"Sure. Good night."

She watched as Tim pulled carefully out of the driveway and headed down the street. She watched his taillights disappear, then she ran across the lawn to the front door. She leapt over the final few feet and sailed through the air to land on the welcome mat. She had a genuine date with Tim Cooper—at last!

* * *

The gossip on Thursday was hot and furious. Could it be true that Tim Cooper had asked Brittany Tate to the Winter Carnival Ball? Had Brittany really reformed? Had Samantha Daley tired of Kyle Kirkwood already, and had she stolen Mark Giordano away from Chris Martinez?

Robin rested her head on the table at lunch. "I'm exhausted. I can't gossip one more minute," she mumbled. "And I can't eat. My lips need a rest."

Calvin, Niles, and Nikki laughed. Even Lacey smiled.

Robin's head lifted once again, though. Her plastic shark earrings danced as she shook her head. "But—did you hear the latest? Kyle Kirkwood asked Chris Martinez to the dance."

"And when everyone's not talking about who's going with whom, they're talking about clothes," Nikki said. "Everybody I talked to is trying to come up with a fabulous outfit for the fifties bowling party on Friday night."

"I hear that Karen Jacobs has a poodle skirt," Robin said. "I'm so jealous."

Calvin grinned. "What are you worried about, Fisher? You always steal the show."

"I'm afraid I'm out of luck," Niles said. "I didn't bring any suitable clothes."

"Niles, no matter what you wear, you look classy," Robin said.

"You can just wear your jeans," Nikki advised Niles. "And slick your hair back. You'll be fine."

"What about you, Lacey?" Calvin asked.

"I'm not going," Lacey answered. "I'd rather stay with Rick Friday night. I will go to the dance on Saturday."

"Well, at least we got you to do that," Nikki said. "That's something."

"I wish I didn't feel so guilty about it," Lacey said. She nervously plucked at her notebook with her thin, pale fingers.

Calvin peered over their heads at the far side of the cafeteria. "Look at Ben," he said. "The thicker the clouds get outside, the worse he looks."

Everyone turned to study Ben Newhouse. He was standing by the window, holding a can of soda and frowning. All he'd done that day was worry out loud about the weather. Karen stood next to him, looking up at the sky with him.

"What if it rains?" Ben asked her, sighing. "I'm fresh out of ideas. We'll have to cancel the miniature golf contest, the cross-country race, and the tennis matches."

Karen continued to stare outside. Bare branches scraped against a bleak gray sky.

Things didn't look promising. And the temperature was dropping. "It won't rain," she said uneasily. "I won't let it. If it does, we'll figure something out."

Ben reached over and brushed a strand of light brown hair off her forehead. He smiled. "I can't wait for tomorrow night," he said. "Are you ready to dance the night away?"

"You bet," she said. But what about Saturday night? she was dying to ask. Ben still hadn't mentioned Emily's visit. Of course, he must know she was coming to the Winter Carnival Ball. Karen wished she could ask him about it, as Ellen had advised, but she just couldn't. She couldn't ask Ben if he was still in love with Emily Van Patten. She was too afraid of the answer.

Friday morning Brittany woke up with the satisfying feeling that she was the most prepared she'd ever been for a school project. There was no way she'd disappoint Tim.

The weather was chilly so she dressed in black wool pants, a crisp white shirt, and a black and white tweed jacket. She gathered her hair in a soft ponytail with a silver clip. She looked very serious, Brittany decided as she added a touch of red gloss to her lips. Not the type of girl who schemed or flirted or played with boys' emotions. Brittany grinned at herself in the mirror. But she still looked gorgeous!

The day seemed to drag on forever, but finally last period did arrive. Brittany barely paid attention to the other projects. She and Tim were the last scheduled presentation, and she secretly went over her notes instead of listening.

When their turn came Brittany felt a flutter of nervousness, which she soon forgot as they began.

They'd rehearsed their presentation the night before in a marathon session on the phone. The preparation paid off. Neither one of them made one mistake, and their enthusiasm fired up the rest of the class. Mr. Greene and Ms. Marshall beamed at them from the back of the room.

When the final bell rang Brittany wanted to throw her arms around Tim, but Mr. Greene came over just then. He told Brittany that she'd really impressed him. She had the editor in chief position locked up!

The rest of the class gathered their books, already buzzing about the bowling party that night. Tim turned toward her, his eyes shining.

"That was fantastic, partner," he said as the rest of the class filed out. "I think we might have aced the project, thanks to you.

Those tapes went over great." He held out his hand, and she shook it. Tim didn't drop her hand right away. He just kept smiling, his gray eyes warm and appreciative. Brittany couldn't believe it. How long had she waited for Tim to look at her like that?

Finally Tim dropped her hand. "Well, I'd better get going. I'll see you at the bowling party tonight, and then I'll pick you up at seven-thirty for the dance tomorrow, right?"

"Perfect," Brittany said.

"Do you want to go to the country club or the Loft afterward? I hear Kim and Jeremy are going to the country club, so . . ."

Tim's voice trailed off. He was being polite, Brittany knew. Kim and Jeremy weren't his favorite people.

"Let's go to the Loft," Brittany said with a mischievous smile.

She was rewarded by a dazzling smile from Tim. "Great. Well, I'll see you tonight, then."

Brittany watched Tim leave, feeling so happy that she was ready to burst. Everything was going her way—finally. Maybe there *was* something in being nice all the time. She couldn't wait for that night. She'd be sweet to the whole junior class, including that super-nerd, Paul Kelly, if it meant Tim Cooper would look at her like that again.

* * *

That night Nikki, Niles, Calvin, and Robin all went to the bowling party at Mel's Lanes together. When they walked in old rock 'n' roll music was blasting, and everyone was transformed into fifties teenagers in full skirts, short pants, saddle shoes, ponytails, and ducktails.

When Niles and Calvin went off to find sodas Robin turned to Nikki. "This is fun!" she said, her dark eyes sparkling. She was wearing rolled-up jeans, a white T-shirt, and a black leather motorcycle jacket. She had slicked back her hair like a boy's. She and Niles had burst out laughing when they saw each other. They'd worn the same outfit.

"I'm glad I'm not in the bowling tournament," Nikki said over the crash of pins. "I'd much rather dance with Niles."

"I'm glad he finally kissed you," Robin said. "I was about to die from the suspense."

"Me, too," Nikki agreed.

"Besides, you're dressed for dancing, not bowling," Robin observed. "Where did you get that cool dress?"

"My mom saved it," Nikki said. "She wore it in high school." Her dress was pale green with bright pink flowers. Nikki was wearing a stiff petticoat underneath it so that the skirt rustled.

Robin sighed. "I can't believe Tim asked Brittany to the dance. Kim rushed up to me yesterday to rub the news in my face. I'm sure she's hoping you'll cry in your pillow all night, Nikki.''

"I don't know what makes her think that," Nikki said, fingering the end of her ponytail. "I'm with Niles, and I couldn't be happier."

"Right," Robin said.

"My main concern these days," Nikki said as they drifted toward the dance floor, "is Gillian. When is she coming? *Why* is she coming? She's the one who told Niles they should see other people. It's driving me crazy."

Just as they reached the dance floor they saw Tim and Brittany. Nikki stopped dead in her tracks as she watched Tim slide his arm around Brittany's waist.

Nikki turned away quickly, and Robin cleared her throat. "I could be way off base here, Nikki," she said. "And you can tell me I'm crazy if you want."

"You're crazy," Nikki said.

"Hey, I didn't say anything yet!"

Nikki grinned. "I know."

"Very funny. Anyway, I've been thinking about this Gillian thing. And I think that maybe—just maybe—it's a smoke screen."

Nikki frowned. "A smoke screen? What does that mean?"

"Well," Robin said, "all this wondering if Niles is in love with his old girlfriend could just be your way to distract yourself from something you don't want to face."

"What's that?" Nikki asked. She followed Robin's finger pointing back to the dance floor. Brittany was smiling up at Tim, her dark eyes shining. She was wearing a pink skirt cinched with a wide belt that made her waist look tiny.

Robin took a deep breath. "That *you* might be the one who's still in love with your old flame," she said calmly.

11 ～～～

After Brittany's dance with Tim was over she saw Kyle Kirkwood standing by the bowling balls, talking to his friend Greg Hazen. Kyle had played a small part in her scheme, even though he wasn't aware of it. Brittany decided to be nice to him.

"Kyle, thanks so much for telling me about the oral history foundation," she said. "You were great to tell me about the place."

"I really liked your presentation," Kyle said. "I learned a lot."

"I'm glad. And I learned a lot from yours, too," Brittany said politely. She had barely paid attention to Kyle's boring project, but Kyle deserved some praise. If it hadn't been for him, she might not be going to the Winter

Carnival Ball with Tim Cooper! She could almost kiss him. Brittany smiled her lush, generous smile at him.

But what Brittany didn't know was that she was being observed. Samantha was standing behind a pillar, straining to see Kyle without being seen. She couldn't believe it. There was Brittany, leaning closer and closer to Kyle. Brittany looked as if she was about to kiss him!

How could Brittany do this to her? Samantha had given up pursuing Tim. She'd left him alone and gone after Mark Giordano instead. Was Brittany this cruel? It made Samantha long for that boring, goody-goody Brittany she'd seen all too briefly.

She headed back to the bowling lanes, where some kids were warming up for the tournament. Samantha felt like bursting into tears. She sank onto a bench and stared at her saddle shoes.

She'd never been so miserable in her whole life. She'd spent the entire afternoon hitting tennis ball after tennis ball with Mark so that they'd be ready for the tennis match. Now she remembered why she'd sworn never to date another jock.

She felt like going home right then. She missed Kyle, and she was tired of fighting. She was being outflanked at every turn.

Brittany was a pro. How had Samantha ever expected to win?

The fifties bowling party was a smashing success. By the time Ben and Karen had packed up the tapes and helped Mel, the owner, clean up a little, everyone had left. Karen went for her coat, thinking about the evening. She'd had a great time with Ben. Everyone had complimented her on her outfit, and she and Ben had come in second in the dance contest. Karen should have been happy, but doubts kept nagging at her. She couldn't help thinking about the Winter Carnival Ball. What would happen when Emily showed up?

Suddenly Karen knew that she had to talk to Ben. Now. She couldn't stand the suspense anymore.

Ben was waiting for her by the front door. "It's getting cold," he said. "You'd better button up your coat. Maybe we should have gone back to our winter theme," he said worriedly.

"It'll be okay," Karen assured him. "We planned on everyone wearing down vests and jackets for the tennis and miniature golf events, so it doesn't matter if it's chilly."

"True." Ben opened the car door. "I'm glad Sasha talked me into switching back to the snowflake theme for the ball."

Ben slid behind the wheel and turned to her before he started the car. "Listen, Karen, I'm sorry I've been so obsessed with this carnival. I know I've been kind of a bore. But after tomorrow," he said with a winning smile, "I'll be back to normal." He started the car.

Karen smiled weakly. What is normal? she wanted to ask. Was it a Ben who was as interested in her as she was in him? Or was it a Ben consumed with school activities and pining away for Emily Van Patten?

As Ben drove her home through the dark streets of River Heights Karen shivered, and it wasn't because of the cold night. It was because she was afraid. She couldn't lose Ben!

When he pulled up in her driveway and shut off the lights and the ignition she turned to him.

"Ben, I want to know something. You can be honest with me. How do you feel——"

"Oh, no!" Ben sat straight up, staring over Karen's left shoulder. "No, no, no!"

She tried to twist around. "What is it?"

"It's awful!"

Slowly Karen turned, expecting to see an escaped maniac in her driveway. She peered out into the blackness. "What do you see, Ben?" she hissed.

Ben reached forward and flipped on the

car's headlights. He turned her head forward. Now, in the bright glare, Karen could see what was alarming Ben.

"It's snowing," she said.

The snow started with just a few light flakes, but within an hour it was falling fast and hard. A surprise storm had sped down from Canada, and the weather forecasters were all puzzled at their failure to predict it.

When Lacey woke up Saturday morning the snow had let up, the roads had been plowed, and there was a deep white blanket on the ground. A few flakes still drifted down against a pearl white sky. It was a perfect Winter Carnival day.

Lacey dressed hurriedly, then rushed downstairs. She wanted to spend some time with Rick before heading to the festivities. She almost regretted telling Nikki and Robin that she'd go, but she couldn't back out now. Lacey grabbed a banana for breakfast and headed for the bus.

When she got to the hospital she recognized the Strattons' red Blazer. Lacey's heart fell. She had wanted to be alone with Rick. Even though she knew it was unfair, she couldn't help hoping that Rick's whole family wasn't there.

Only Mrs. Stratton was by his bedside

when Lacey pushed open the door to Rick's room. Lacey began to smile a hello when she noticed that Mrs. Stratton's eyes were red-rimmed.

"Is something wrong?" Lacey ran to Rick's bedside. "Is Rick worse?"

"No," Mrs. Stratton said. "He's not worse. But he's not any better, either. And according to the doctors, it isn't a good sign."

Mrs. Stratton sounded bone tired and sad. Lacey was used to her optimism and cheerfulness, and this new tone frightened her.

She grabbed Mrs. Stratton's hand and squeezed it. "I don't care what the doctors say," she said urgently. "He's going to get better. He is!"

Lacey got up and went to stand beside Rick. She looked down at his face and smiled. "You know how determined he is, Mrs. Stratton. There isn't anything he won't try."

Mrs. Stratton nodded slowly. "You're right, Lacey. I'll just have to keep remembering that. It's just so hard seeing him this way."

"I know. But we have to try." Lacey stood, holding Rick's hand, her red hair waving around her thin, fierce face.

Mrs. Stratton began to smile. "I don't

know what I would have done without you, Lacey," she said. "You've been such a help to me."

"Please, Mrs. Stratton. Don't say that. I—"

"No, I mean it. Seeing you sit here day after day, seeing your faith, your trust that Rick will recover—well, it's given me hope, too. I just wanted you to know that."

Tears began to slip down Lacey's cheeks. "Please stop," she said hoarsely. "You don't understand."

Mrs. Stratton looked concerned. "What is it, Lacey? Have I upset you?"

Just say it, Robin would have advised. Open your mouth, and you'll find the words. Lacey took a deep breath. She dropped Rick's hand.

"You see, Mrs. Stratton," she said, choking on the words, "I have no right to be here. I'm the reason Rick fell off the rocks that day."

Mrs. Stratton looked startled. "Lacey, what do you mean?"

Tears falling down her face, Lacey sobbed out the whole story. Once she'd started she couldn't stop. She cried and cried as she told Rick's mother how she'd mistrusted him, how he'd driven off so angrily.

"I can't forgive myself," she said. "And I

don't blame you for not forgiving me either. I'll just leave now."

"Lacey, wait a minute." Gently Mrs. Stratton pushed a stray lock of hair off Lacey's forehead. "Honey, I understand how you feel, but I don't blame you one little bit. You aren't responsible for Rick's being here."

"You don't have to say that, Mrs. Stratton."

"But I mean it! The day of Rick's accident I yelled at him for something after school. Oh, it wasn't important, but I was frazzled and rushed, and I yelled at him. I know that he was angry. So I've been sitting here feeling guilty, too. Isn't that strange?"

"Really?" Lacey asked. She guessed Mrs. Stratton was trying to make her feel better. But it only helped a little bit. "But that's silly."

"That's just my point," Mrs. Stratton said. "When something happens to someone we love we think of all the ways we might have failed them. Times that we were impatient or unkind. We have too much time, sitting here, to think about those things." Mrs. Stratton's gaze drifted over to Rick, and her eyes were full of pain.

She shook herself slightly and turned back to Lacey. "You can't blame yourself, honey. So please don't feel guilty, Lacey. I know you love Rick, and I'm sure he loves you, too. That's what's really important."

"Thank you," Lacey whispered.

"Now," Mrs. Stratton said briskly, "today is Winter Carnival, isn't it? You should go have some fun with your friends."

Lacey shook her head. "I don't know if I can."

"Try. Maybe it will take your mind off things for a little while. I'll sit with Rick."

Lacey nodded and smiled at Mrs. Stratton. She did feel a little better now that she knew Mrs. Stratton didn't blame her. But as she leaned over to kiss Rick goodbye and felt his cold cheek she knew that it didn't really matter. She still blamed herself.

Samantha sat on a bench at the country club. All around her kids were joking and laughing. But she was filled with dread. She had to compete in a skating race instead of a tennis match.

She couldn't believe it. Tennis she could handle. But a skating relay? She couldn't skate to save her life!

A panicked Ben Newhouse had woken her up that morning with the news. Tennis was out because of the snow. Moon Lake wasn't frozen enough, but the country club had flooded its tennis courts the night before.

They were completely frozen, Ben had babbled, smooth and glassy. So all of the mixed doubles tennis teams would be skating relay teams instead.

Samantha had tried to tell him that her ankles were rubber on the ice and she sat on it more than she glided over it. But Ben hadn't listened. He'd just said, "You'll be terrific, trust me," and hung up.

Now, sitting on a bench beside the ice, Samantha watched the other racers warm up. Some of them were terrific. She'd come to the club an hour early to practice with Mark, and her ankles were already tired. At least she hadn't made a complete fool of herself. But staying on her feet and racing were two different things.

"You don't look very happy."

Samantha shaded her eyes against the glare. Brittany was standing in front of her, grinning.

"Don't you know it's carnival day?" Brittany said, flopping down beside her. "You look as if you're ready for a funeral instead. What's up?"

Samantha regarded the tips of her skates. She couldn't believe even Brittany could be so mean. Not only had she ground Samantha into the mud, but she had Tim *and* Kyle— and now she had the nerve to gloat.

"Brittany, let's just have a truce, okay?" Samantha burst out. "I can't stand this anymore."

Brittany frowned. "Stand what?"

"I'm sorry I flirted with Tim Cooper. I apologize. Even though you said you didn't want him, I should have known you didn't mean it. And anyway, I only did it to make Kyle jealous. So please stop flirting with Kyle. You made your point. You won."

"Kyle? I'm flirting with Kyle Kirkwood?" A puzzled look crossed Brittany's face.

What an actress, Samantha thought bitterly. "Oh, come on, Brittany," she said impatiently. "As long as I'm coming clean, you should, too. Just drop the innocent act, okay?"

"Samantha, I swear I don't know what you're talking about. I thought you were through with Kyle. Are you serious about him?"

Samantha gave her an exasperated look. "You know very well that I am, Brittany. You've been all over him because of it. Well, you paid me back, so I give up. Now will you please leave Kyle alone?"

"Sam, the only reason I was talking to Kyle was to learn about the oral history foundation."

Angrily, Samantha pulled on her hot pink mittens. "Mrs. Daley didn't raise a fool,

Brittany. Can't you think of a better excuse than that? Do you really expect me to believe that?" She struggled to her feet. "I can't believe you're still pulling this innocent-angel act. Excuse me, please. I've got a race to skate." With great dignity Samantha glided onto the ice. Immediately her feet flew out from under her, and she landed in a heap on the ice.

Brittany watched Samantha fall, but she didn't laugh. She bit her lip and quickly got up and walked away.

It didn't take her long to find Kyle. He was sitting with Chris Martinez. She was telling him about the last River Heights High football game, and he seemed to be bored to death.

"Kyle," Brittany said, "can I see you a minute?"

"Sure," Kyle said eagerly, getting up.

"Listen, Kyle," Brittany said as soon as they were out of earshot, "I'm going to butt in on this thing with you and Samantha."

Kyle scowled. "What thing? There *is* no thing, at least as far as Samantha is concerned."

Brittany waved her hand. "I'm going to give you a piece of advice, and then I'll leave you alone. Samantha always hides her real feelings. She can't help it. She was taught that you can never tell a boy how you really feel. So if she tells you she doesn't care about you, then you know for sure she does. If she tells you she never wants to see you again, she's dying for you. When you have to start worrying is when she tells you she adores you. That means she couldn't care less."

Kyle grinned. "That's my Sam."

"Exactly. So my advice is, if you're interested, don't give up."

"Oh, I haven't given up," Kyle said with a shrug. "I've just been taking a breather."

"I wouldn't wait too long," Brittany advised. "I mean, look what happened to Scarlett and Rhett."

12

"Skaters, take your marks!" Ben shouted.

Samantha watched as Mark bent over. He played hockey, so he was a good skater. He'd be the first racer. Then came Karen Jacobs, then Martin Salko. Samantha had begged to be able to go last, and Mark had given in. Usually the fastest skater was last, but Samantha was sure that Karen, Mark, and Martin would give her a big lead. That was the only way, she decided, that she wouldn't make a fool of herself.

"Get set, go!" Ben shouted, and the skaters took off. Mark bent over, his muscular legs pumping furiously. Samantha saw Chris Martinez on the sidelines watching him. Next to her was Kyle.

Kyle looked cute in a bulky turtleneck and

denim jacket. Samantha felt so awful she began to question her behavior. Maybe Kyle did have a point about her being friends with his friends. Maybe it wasn't right to expect him to drop out of his crowd and become part of hers.

Mark rounded the rink, made an expert turn around an orange cone, and started back. The crowd was screaming and cheering. Even the entrants in the snow sculpture competition had left their designs and were on the sidelines yelling.

Mark was the first one back, and then Karen took off. She was a good skater, and their lead widened. By the time Martin was tagged and began to skate Samantha relaxed a bit. Even *she* couldn't mess up this lead.

Too soon, she saw Martin heading toward her fast. This was it. Samantha took several deep breaths. The noise of the crowd was in her ears, and she felt dazzled by the sun on the snow. She prayed she wouldn't make a fool of herself. And then Martin was there, tagging her hand, and she was off, flying down the ice.

She had a comfortable lead, so she tried to concentrate on keeping her balance rather than going too fast.

She saw Kyle out of the corner of her eye as she passed. He was saying something to

Chris, who was smiling and laughing. He was making fun of her!

Grimly, Samantha sped up her pace. She'd win the race and show Chris Martinez who the athlete was! She was flying now, her curls bobbing along behind her, bent over as Mark had taught her. She was winning—she had kept the lead!

The orange cone was just ahead of her. Mark had told her to try to get as close as she could on her turn. Samantha zoomed toward the cone. But somehow, though she was aiming to miss it, she hit it straight on. A very surprised Samantha found herself in the air. She seemed to hang there for a second, then sailed headfirst into a snowbank at the end of the rink.

Laughter exploded from the sidelines as Samantha struggled to extricate herself from the soft mound of snow. Then she saw a leather glove in front of her face. At least there was one gentleman in the crowd. Samantha looked up into a pair of twinkling brown eyes.

"I think you need a hand," Kyle said with a grin.

Grudgingly Samantha grabbed Kyle's hand. She was surprised at how strong he was. He hauled her out of the snowbank easily.

Behind them the crowd was cheering as Erik Neilson won the race for the B team. "I guess I lost the race," Samantha said woefully.

"But you did it with style," Kyle said, smiling.

Samantha pulled away. "Don't you have to get back to Christina?" she said with a sniff.

"In a minute." Kyle just stood there, still smiling. "Don't you think this has gone on long enough?" he asked.

"What has gone on long enough?" Samantha brushed off the seat of her pants.

"Trying to make me jealous."

"I don't know what you're talking about," Samantha said loftily.

"I'm talking about Tim Cooper and Mark Giordano," Kyle said. "Samantha, you can't pull that stuff on someone like me. You can flirt all you want, but I'm not going to let you manipulate me."

Her flirting *had* worked! Kyle had noticed. And he *was* jealous, no matter what he said. Samantha would have jumped for joy, but she'd probably fall down again. "I didn't think you noticed," she said.

"Of course I noticed. But I'm not going to let you get away with it."

"But what if I really *am* interested in Mark?" Samantha asked coyly.

Kyle shrugged. "Then I won't suggest what I'm about to."

"What's that?" Samantha asked. She tried to look as though she couldn't care one way or another.

"That we go to the dance together tonight." Kyle looked at her, his brown eyes serious now. "I've missed you, Samantha," he said softly. "I'm probably crazy to tell you that, but I did."

Warmth stole back into Samantha's fingers and toes, even though she was still freezing. "Oh, Kyle, I missed you, too. I'd love to go to the dance with you tonight." She hesitated. "But what about Mark?" she asked suddenly. "I can't stand him up."

Kyle grinned. "Why do you think I asked Chris to the ball? I think we can convince them to switch partners. We'd be doing a good deed—they're still crazy about each other."

"Wait a minute. You mean you only asked Chris because I was going with Mark?"

"Well, she's nice, too," Kyle said. "But, yes, I asked Chris because I figured that way I could get to dance with you the whole night. I had a feeling that Mark and Chris would make up soon."

"Why, Kyle Kirkwood, how dare you!" Samantha exclaimed. "You planned this all along! You let me run after Mark Giordano and make a fool of myself on this skating rink, just to make you jealous. And you knew it all the time. You *snake!*"

"That's about right," Kyle said, satisfied. "I knew we'd end up together."

Abruptly, Samantha turned around to stalk off. But she forgot she still had her skates on, and she almost pitched forward onto the ice again. Kyle's hand shot out to steady her.

"I hate you, Kyle Kirkwood," she muttered through gritted teeth.

"That's what I want to hear." Kyle drew her closer to him.

"I despise you!"

"Terrific." He slipped his arms around her.

"You're a low-down, dirty skunk, and I will never, ever forgive you!"

Kyle leaned forward and kissed her. His lips were warm against hers, and she felt him smile.

"I'm crazy about you, too, Sam," he said.

That night the gym was a fairyland. Sasha and her decorating committee had strung tiny white lights in bunches, and they twinkled overhead like hard white stars. As a final touch, one whole brick wall had been covered in midnight blue paper and strewn with silver paper cutouts of stars and snowflakes.

The gym was already crowded when Nikki and Niles arrived. Mr. Greene and Ms. Marshall, the chaperons, were standing together and talking. Robin was dancing with Calvin, her ice-blue dress shimmering under the lights. Everyone in their silks and velvets seemed to sparkle and glow.

Nikki felt as though she were floating. Niles was so handsome in a light gray suit, and he had loved her new silver dress. There were tiny metallic threads sewn into the skirt, which glittered under the tiny lights. Nikki felt as though nothing could spoil that night. It was truly magical. Then, over Niles's shoulder, she saw Tim and Brittany arrive.

Tim looked fantastic in a dark blue suit, and Brittany attracted every eye in the gym in her ruby-colored velvet dress. She was wearing ruby satin shoes, and her dark hair was swept up with a rhinestone clip in the shape of a snowflake. She looked both sophisticated and sexy.

Nikki turned back to Niles quickly. "There's Sasha," she said. "Let's go tell her how fantastic the gym looks."

They walked over to Sasha, who was wearing black, as usual. That night her dress was of shimmering silk, and there was a gardenia in her black hair, which she had shaped into a cap instead of spikes.

"You look great," Nikki told her. "And the gym does, too. I hardly recognize it."

"It's quite a job," Niles chimed in. "I never thought a gymnasium could be so elegant."

"Thanks," Sasha said. "I was afraid we wouldn't be able to pull it off in the end. Ben had me working on a tropical theme for days. The art supply closet is stuffed with leis and palm trees. I think we've got to have some kind of tropical dance soon!"

Nikki and Niles laughed, and the band kicked in with "Winter Wonderland." Niles swept Nikki onto the dance floor, and they whirled underneath the twinkling white lights, Nikki's silver skirt swirling around her.

Nikki turned her head and snuggled closer to Niles. So what if Brittany looked fabulous? So what if she and Tim became a couple? She was in love with Niles, and she wasn't going to think about what the future would bring.

Niles swung her around. "I'm wild about you, Nikki Masters," he said, his dark eyes glowing.

"And I'm wild about you," Nikki said.

Behind Niles Tim slipped his arm around Brittany, and they began to dance.

Ben took Karen's hand and led her away from all the kids who were congratulating them on the fantastic success of the Winter Carnival.

"If I hear the words *Winter Carnival* one more time, I'll scream," he said to her. "Now I just want to have fun. Let's dance." He squeezed her hand. "You so look great, Karen. You're the prettiest girl here."

That's because Emily Van Patten hasn't arrived yet, Karen thought sourly as she followed Ben onto the dance floor. Usually a compliment from Ben would make her melt. But she didn't feel pretty, and she wouldn't feel good until she knew for sure that Ben really loved her.

Ben pulled away a couple of inches to look at her. "Is something wrong, Karen?" he asked. "It seems as if you have something on your mind."

Karen nodded, biting her lip.

"Tell me." He squeezed her hand. "Is it about the *Record*? Did Brittany steal your notes for a story again?"

Karen shook her head. "No. Brittany's a whole new person, remember? It's about us, Ben."

"Us?"

"I was wondering—I was wondering what —well, what you thought about me."

"You're wonderful," Ben said promptly. He gave a relieved laugh. "Is that all?"

"Well, no." This was even harder than she'd thought. "How do you really feel about me, Ben?" she burst out. "I mean, do you care about me?"

"Of course I—"

"I love you, Ben." Horrified, Karen heard the words leave her mouth as though they'd been spoken by somebody else. She hadn't meant to say that! How could she have let that slip?

Ben stopped dancing and became kind of stiff. "Maybe we should sit down," he said.

Numbly, Karen followed him off the dance floor. He led her to a shadowy corner, where he pulled out chairs for both of them to sit down. Karen braced herself. What was Ben going to say?

"I care about you very much, Karen," he said slowly. "I think you're a terrific person, and—"

"It's okay, Ben. You don't have to say any more," Karen broke in. She felt so ashamed she could die. Obviously Ben didn't feel the same way about her. He had a pained, embarrassed expression on his face.

"No, I want to say something," Ben said. He took both of her hands in his. "Look. I don't know how I feel, exactly. I've just come out of a steady relationship, and I wasn't looking for a steady girlfriend again right away. But then things started happening between us. Karen, I do know I want to keep seeing you. I know I care about you."

Care. Karen heard the word numbly. It was so inadequate compared to love. Ben was obviously trying to be nice, but she couldn't stand to hear another word. She was ready to burst into tears, and that would make things even worse.

Just then Karen heard excited cries coming from behind them. The music had stopped, and she could hear girls squealing. Karen twisted around and saw a group gathering.

"What is it?" she asked Ben. She was grateful for the diversion.

Ben gave a start. "Emily's here," he said.

The crowd parted, and Karen saw that Emily Van Patten was standing in the middle of it. She was wearing a strapless white velvet dress, and she looked beautiful, tall and blond and self-assured.

"I'd better say hello," Ben said. He turned to her. "I know it's a bad time, but it will look funny if I don't."

"Of course you should," Karen said firmly. She felt tears gather behind her eyes. "I'm just going to go to the girls' room." So she could find an empty stall where she could cry her eyes out—or maybe bang her head against the wall.

She watched, with tears pooled in her eyes, as Ben crossed the gym to Emily's side. Emily smiled when she saw him, and she stepped into his arms for a hug. That was all Karen needed to see. Stifling a sob, she ran quickly across the gym toward the girls' room.

13

Robin told Calvin she'd be right back and went off to find Lacey, whom she found behind the refreshment table.

"Hi," Lacey greeted her. "You look great. I love your dress."

"Thanks," Robin said. She studied her friend.

Lacey looked pale and distracted. She was wearing a black skirt and fancy ruffled blouse, but it was obvious she hadn't cared about what she wore. She had skipped make-up, but her long red hair was held neatly off her forehead by a silver headband, and tiny silver earrings were in her ears.

"How's it going, kid?" Robin asked.

Lacey shrugged and moved down the table, away from the people waiting for punch. "All right, I guess. Rick's still the same. But I did finally tell Mrs. Stratton that I felt Rick's accident was my fault."

"What did she say?"

"She said it wasn't. Just as you and Nikki said."

"Well, it's a majority opinion, then," Robin said lightly, but Lacey didn't smile. "Lacey, doesn't that make you feel any better at all?"

"I don't think I'll feel better until Rick wakes up. Tonight for the first time I keep thinking he might not."

Robin's heart went out to her friend. Lacey had suffered so much, and there was nothing Robin could do except be there for her.

"He'll get better, Lacey. You have to keep believing. You can't stop now."

Lacey nodded, but she didn't look convinced. "I shouldn't be here. I should be with Rick."

"Just hang in there," Robin said.

Lacey smiled. "Thanks, Rob. Now go back and dance with Cal. I'll be fine."

"Okay," Robin said reluctantly. She turned away from Lacey and sighed as she headed back toward Cal. Just then Robin saw Brittany whisper something to Tim. Suddenly Brittany headed across the floor toward the girls' room.

Grimly, Robin set her shoulders. She'd been debating whether or not to confront

Brittany. Lacey's pain had convinced her— it was time to corner Brittany and let her have it.

Robin stepped up her pace and grabbed Brittany's elbow right outside the double doors of the hall.

"Hey," Brittany said in surprise. "What are you doing, Robin? That hurts."

Determinedly, Robin dragged Brittany a little way down the darkened hall.

"What are you doing? Cut that out." Brittany struggled to free herself from Robin's grip.

"I'd come along if I were you, Brittany. I don't think you want anyone to overhear us," Robin warned.

"I don't care," Brittany said angrily. "I'm not going to stand here and—"

"Be quiet, Brittany," Robin snapped. "Because I don't want you to miss one single word of what I have to say."

"Really, Robin," Brittany said. "Cut the drama. I was on my way to—"

"I don't care," Robin interrupted fiercely. "I have something to say. I've seen you do some cruel things, Brittany. I've seen you steal boyfriends, and I've seen you lie. But I didn't think even you were capable of this."

Brittany backed away toward the wall. "I don't know what you're talking about," she said.

"You lied to Lacey," Robin said flatly. "You told her that Rick might be involved in that cheating scandal."

Brittany tossed her head. "So what if I repeated one tiny rumor to Lacey?"

"So what?" Robin took a step closer to her. "So Rick Stratton is in the hospital. You wanted them to fight, and they did. Rick went off rock climbing and had an accident, and you're the reason he's in the hospital!"

"That's ridiculous," Brittany said nervously.

"Could it be that you feel guilty?" Robin went on. "Is that why you tried to be good for the past few days? It didn't work, did it, Brittany? You might have fooled Tim, but you didn't fool anybody else."

"You're really jumping to conclusions, Robin," Brittany said shrilly. "Why would I want to hurt Lacey? I never even think about her."

"But she knew about that old junkheap of a car you had," Robin said. "You started this big campaign to get the school to haul it off the lot when you were the owner the whole time! And Lacey found out about it."

"Yes, and Lacey blackmailed me," Brittany said.

"Only because you had lied to Tim about Nikki. So don't tell me you didn't have anything against Lacey. I'm sure you were just waiting for the opportunity to get her back. But I want you to know something, Brittany Tate. This isn't some little scheme to get a boy to ask you out, or to get a scoop in the *Record*. This is Rick's life we're talking about."

"Listen, Robin, I—"

"Don't bother trying to excuse yourself, Brittany," Robin snapped. "There is no excuse. You can try for the next fifty years to be a good person, but you'll never make it."

Robin turned away and headed down the dark hall. Brittany took a deep breath. She smoothed her hair and tried to fasten her rhinestone clip more firmly, but her hands were shaking. Tim must be wondering where she was. She turned around and saw Tim standing just a few feet away in the shadows.

Brittany flushed, and she was glad she was in dim light. She prayed that Tim hadn't heard anything. She couldn't see his face. What was he thinking? "Tim, what are you doing here? Did you miss me?" she asked in a teasing tone.

"Don't bother, Brittany." Tim's tone was flat. "I heard everything."

He stepped out into the light, and she saw the angry expression on his face. Brittany's heart sank all the way down to her new shoes. She didn't know if any amount of fast talking could save her this time. Tim had obviously had it with her. She'd never forgive Robin as long as she lived!

Ellen Ming pushed open the door to the girls' room. She went down the row of stalls until she recognized a pair of feet. She knocked softly on the door. She'd seen Karen dash out of the gym as everyone's attention focused on Emily and Ben. She knew her friend was upset.

"Karen, it's me, Ellen. Let me in, okay?"

"Is there anybody else in here?" Karen whispered.

"No," Ellen said as she squeezed inside. She gazed sympathetically at her friend's tearstained face. "I saw Emily Van Patten."

Karen nodded. "She looked gorgeous. I just wanted to die, Ellen!"

"Why?" Ellen asked. "Everything's okay with Ben, isn't it? Didn't you talk to him?"

"Oh, I talked to him all right," Karen said bitterly. "And I said the worst possible thing. I told him I loved him!" Karen started to cry again. "And he doesn't love me!" she wailed. "How could I be so stupid?"

Ellen frowned. "What did he say?"

"He said he *cared,*" Karen said in a disgusted tone.

"But that's good," Ellen said. "Ben is just coming out of going steady with Emily. He might not be sure of his feelings for you yet. But that doesn't mean his feelings can't grow."

"That's what Ben said." Karen sniffled.

"You see? Here," Ellen said, handing her some toilet tissue. "Dry your face and splash some cold water on it. Fight for Ben! Emily lives in New York, and you live here. So hang in there. Something's got to go right for *somebody* around here."

"What do you mean?" Karen asked, drying her eyes.

"Nothing," Ellen assured her. She gave a strained smile.

"Oh, Ellen, you're right. I can't hide in here all night." Hurriedly Karen wiped her face, then went to the sink.

Ellen watched Karen fix her makeup. She could tell Karen what to do, no problem. Why couldn't she give herself advice? Her own problem was eating her up inside. And she couldn't talk to *anybody* about it—no matter how miserable she was!

Samantha couldn't believe how well everything was working out. Mark and Chris were glued together on the dance floor. Both of them were ecstatic that somebody had stepped in and forced them to make up. And she had danced every dance with Kyle.

"Do you want a soda?" Kyle asked.

"Sounds great. All that dancing made me thirsty," Samantha said.

As they walked arm in arm to the refreshment table Samantha saw that Greg and Belinda were in line there. Next to them stood Kim and Jeremy. Samantha glanced nervously at Kyle, but he hadn't said anything more to her about his friends, and she'd been hoping the problem would just go away.

Kim looked at Samantha, then at Kyle. When he turned away to get the sodas she leaned toward Samantha. "I thought your date was Mark Giordano," she whispered loudly. "What are you doing with Kyle? I thought you dropped him."

Kyle turned around. Samantha could see by his face that he'd heard every word. Kim's "whisper" could probably be heard all the way to Chicago.

"We got back together," Samantha said.

Kim shrugged. "Well, come sit at our table, then. Now that you're not with Mark, you don't have to hang out with the jocks all night."

Samantha didn't hesitate. "Actually, Kim," she said firmly, "Kyle and I are going to sit with his friends tonight." She slipped her arm into Kyle's and smiled into his honey brown eyes. "Let's go sit with Greg and Belinda, Kyle," she said.

A slow, dazzling smile broke out on Kyle's face. "Sure, Samantha," he said. "Let's go."

Karen looked everywhere. Ben was not to be found. Where had he gone? Was he angry at her for staying away so long? Karen searched the crowd with frantic eyes while trying to appear calm. Why, oh why did she ever have that talk with Ben?

She was craning her neck when Cheryl Worth bumped right into her.

"Whoops, sorry, Karen," Cheryl apologized. "I didn't see you. I'm looking for Emily. Have you seen her?"

Dread settled in Karen's stomach. "Not for a while," she forced out. "Is she missing?"

"I haven't seen her for ages," Cheryl said, her eyes searching the room. "She promised to tell me all about New York. I'm going there during spring break with my parents. She knows all the hot places to go."

"That's nice," Karen said automatically. But her heart was beating in fear. Ben was missing. Emily was missing. It didn't take Sherlock Holmes to figure out these mysterious disappearances. Emily and Ben had sneaked off somewhere together!

If Lacey had to pour one more soda, she'd turn over the whole refreshment table. She tried to smile as the people crowded around, jostling and laughing, but she knew it was no use. If the refreshment committee wasn't so shorthanded, she'd slip away and go home, but nobody except Lacey had volunteered to serve refreshments.

Suddenly she saw Ben Newhouse pushing through the crowd. His concerned eyes met Lacey's.

"Rick," she whispered. She knocked several glasses of soda all over the table.

"Watch out, Lacey!" Lara Bennett cried.

Lacey threw a pile of napkins at the huge pool of soda. Ben reached her side and drew her away from the table.

"It's Rick, isn't it, Ben?" she asked, searching his face with anxious eyes. "Tell me quickly. Something's happened!" A sob broke loose from her.

"It's all right, Lacey," Ben said rapidly. "He's awake!"

Relief flooded through Lacey, and she slumped against the wall. "He's awake," she repeated numbly.

"Mrs. Stratton called here trying to reach you," Ben continued. "Rick asked for you."

Rick was asking for her. The one night when she wasn't there he'd regained consciousness. When he'd needed her she wasn't there. Again. Lacey's eyes filled with tears.

"Lacey, it's okay. He's fine." Ben took her arm. "I can take you to the hospital if you like."

"I'll get my coat," Lacey whispered. She ran toward the coatroom. Her hands were shaking as she struggled into her coat. Her mind raced over what would happen when she reached the hospital. She prayed that Rick would still be conscious. Would he be glad to see her? Or had he asked for her only to tell her that he never wanted to see her again?

———————————

Brittany is finally a member of the country club, but will dating super snob Chip Worthington help crown her queen of the social scene? Ellen Ming's father has been accused of embezzling by Kim Bishop's father, and Kim isn't about to let her forget. Will Ellen ever be able to face her classmates again? Find out in River Heights #9, *Lies and Whispers*.